Remembrance

Theresa Breslin

At the battlefields in France and Belgium, teenagers wander soberly around the monuments. They push their poppies into the spaces between the stones of the Menin Gate, and the little wooden crosses purchased in Ypres are crowded onto the grave of a young soldier aged fifteen – their age. Nearby runs the Yser Canal where the Canadian John McCrae wrote his poem 'In Flanders Fields'.

At the Somme, around Thiepval and in Beaumont Hamel, they walk through preserved trenches and stand looking into the huge mine craters. By the roadside and on the hills they see cemetery after cemetery, collections of headstones among fields fertile with crops.

The white clay clings, and they spend time wiping boots before reboarding the coach.

'Came over this morning, back home to Britain tonight,' the driver tells me.

One is aware of great lies and great truths, a sudden consciousness of youth and vulnerability and a tremendous sense of loss.

from Theresa Breslin's research notes, 2000

Remembrance

Theresa Breslin

PUFFIN

PUFFIN BOOKS

UK | USA | Canada | Ireland | Australia
India | New Zealand | South Africa

Puffin Books is part of the Penguin Random House group of companies
whose addresses can be found at global.penguinrandomhouse.com.

www.penguin.co.uk www.puffin.co.uk www.ladybird.co.uk

IMPERIAL WAR MUSEUMS

Penguin Random House UK

First published by Doubleday 2002
Published by Corgi Books 2003 and with additional material 2014
Published in this edition 2018
001

Set in 11/16 pt Minion Pro Std
Typeset by Jouve (UK), Milton Keynes
Printed and bound in Great Britain by Clays Ltd, Elcograf S.p.A.

A CIP catalogue record for this book is available from the British Library

ISBN: 978–0–241–35261–8

All correspondence to:
Puffin Books, Penguin Random House Children's
80 Strand, London WC2R 0RL

MIX
Paper from responsible sources
FSC® C018179
FSC www.fsc.org

Penguin Random House is committed to a sustainable future for our business, our readers and our planet. This book is made from Forest Stewardship Council® certified paper.

This book is for Caroline

The author would like to thank
Edith Philip, Assistant Curator,
National War Museum, Edinburgh Castle
George Fraser, Archivist,
Durham Light Infantry Museum
Staff, Lenzie Library
The French and Belgian Tourist Offices
Canadian Visitor Centre, Beaumont-Hamel
In Flanders Fields Museum, Ypres
Imperial War Museum, London
Commonwealth War Graves Commission
Philip Daws – bookseller extraordinaire

The author is grateful for the permission granted to use quotes from the work of Siegfried Sassoon.

A Little Bit of History from IWM (Imperial War Museums)

The First World War caused many changes in British society, and Theresa Breslin's *Remembrance* reflects how life altered for some women. In the years leading up to 1914, women had been vigorously campaigning to be allowed to vote. When war broke out, some women hoped that working for the war effort would prove their value, and persuade the government that women should be given suffrage (the right to vote). But some of the most radical suffragettes took an anti-war viewpoint instead, believing it was wrong to take life. Others saw the war as a political struggle, and refused to help the rich at the expense of the working classes.

At the start of the war, women's work was mostly domestic, such as nursing or charitable fundraising. In *Remembrance*, Charlotte becomes a Voluntary Aid Detachment (or VAD) nurse – a typical activity for upper- or middle-class women who could afford to work for free (as this role was initially unpaid). VADs were first set up in 1909, and gave both men and women basic first-aid training, so they could assist the military medical services in an emergency. As the war continued and more men served overseas, women increasingly filled the gaps they left. Many women worked in their family's business, or stepped into a job to keep it open for a loved one's return. When conscription was introduced in 1916, women became vital to the war effort, and a variety of new jobs became available to them as the war went on. In this story, Maggie moves from shop work, to a munitions factory, to nursing on the Western Front. Many women experienced new jobs as well as a different, freer lifestyle – and some didn't want to give up this newfound freedom once the war had ended.

And, indeed, when the war came to an end in November 1918, there was much less need for female labour. Men returning from the trenches expected to come back to their jobs, so most women had to go back to their traditional domestic roles. Women generally had to resign from their jobs when they got married, as the husband was expected to support them while they looked after the home. But thousands of women had lost their husbands or sweethearts in the conflict, and some of these women needed to work to look after themselves. Others were simply unwilling to return to the life they had before.

Women were granted the right to vote in February 1918, but it didn't extend to everyone and it was not on equal terms with men. Only women over the age of thirty, or those who met certain property criteria, were included. Many younger women – like Charlotte and Maggie – who had toiled in factories, on the land, in the wards, in transportation and all the other occupations they undertook, would not receive the vote until 1928. Yet women had shown what they were capable of, and life would never be quite the same again.

Sarah Paterson, Librarian, IWM

Foreword

by Elizabeth Wein

Like Theresa Breslin, I too was introduced to the agonized and lyrical verse of the Great War when I was about the same age as the young poets who fought and died in it. As a teen, I even wrote some poems for them myself – and set some of their poems to music. I was stunned by the waste of their talent and youth. My understanding of what they were fighting for was so hazy as to be non-existent, but I was fascinated by the broken humanity of the young men in the trenches. I also read and loved Vera Brittain's *Testament of Youth,* so my impression of the war included the nurse's point of view – and even her poetry – alongside the soldiers'.

Remembrance perfectly captures that interlacement of healing and killing, of the connected lives of the wartime generation.

It is an aching paradox that it took the death of so many young men to empower young women. From munitions workers to suffragettes, Theresa Breslin skilfully weaves women's rights into her story. It's an issue that developed along with and even *because of* the war, but which the teenage me took entirely for granted. *Remembrance* shines up this relationship for a new generation: threaded through the horror of senseless killing runs a growing awareness of gender equality, as young women find work and wages and take control of their own lives.

But what I love most about *Remembrance* is its slow burn. Even though the First World War has already started when the story begins, it doesn't yet feel real. Life is still full of picnics and romance and hope for the future. As *Remembrance*'s young men join up and the young women go to work, the reader and the novel's characters are eased into the war at the same time. From the moment when, on the first day of her nursing career, Charlotte uncovers a severed arm in a bucket, the carnage in Europe becomes a physical reality, even in Scotland. First we see the wounded soldiers; then, through John Malcolm's letters, we hear about the horrors of the trenches; finally, slowly but relentlessly, the action moves to France and Belgium, until everyone is knee-deep in mud and blood.

But there is astonishing joy in the intertwined lives of the five young people at the book's heart: Maggie's growing knowledge and broadening worldview, and her increasing understanding of Francis that deepens to love; Francis's dependence on Maggie's sanity to preserve his own; Charlotte's inner core of granite and her infinite kindness; Alex's simple and desperate partnership with the German boy he wounds; and the plainspoken humour and pain in John Malcolm's letters – these form the beating heart of *Remembrance.*

Brightly and painfully, *painfully*, it's a novel that brings the lost generation of a hundred years ago to life.

And yet, when I close this book now, I still do not understand what these young people were made to fight for, any more than fifteen-year-old Alex Dundas does or than I myself did as a teen.

It may be impossible to understand. But this book helps us to *remember.* And that, in the words of the wartime poet Siegfried Sassoon, is a thing we must 'swear by the green of spring'. *Remember them.*

You smug-faced crowds with kindling eye
Who cheer when soldier lads march by,
Sneak home and pray you'll never know
The hell where youth and laughter go.

Siegfried Sassoon
from 'Suicide in the Trenches'

1915

Chapter 1

'IT'S JUST NOT quite *respectable*.'

Charlotte took off her cape, hung it on the hall stand and faced her mother's disapproving look. 'It is a Red Cross uniform, Mother, and we are at war. I'm not trying to look respectable. I'm trying to be *useful*.'

Mrs Armstrong-Barnes frowned. 'It is not just the uniform, Charlotte dear. I dare say you think me old-fashioned, but in my opinion it is not quite seemly to bicycle through the village dressed like that. When *I* was fifteen, young ladies—'

'Mother,' Charlotte interrupted, 'it is a new century and our country is at war. Everyone should help in whatever way they can, and it is quite acceptable now for a young lady to train as a nurse.' Charlotte moved in the direction of the drawing room. 'Has Helen served tea?'

'You are changing the subject,' Charlotte's mother protested as she followed her. 'If you feel the need to help out you could easily become involved in a different type of war work.'

Charlotte knew what her mother had in mind for her, and as they sat down on the sofa together she tried to think of a way to forestall the argument. 'Please accept that this is what I want to do,' she said gently. 'It would not suit me to organize charity functions, I want to contribute in a more direct way, and taking a nursing certificate is a very practical thing to do.'

Her mother gave a little shake of her head. 'It might become *too* practical,' she said. 'One hears things about hospitals . . .'

'Oh, *Mother*,' said Charlotte, pulling off her cap and causing her hair to loosen and fall about her face. 'You have no need to worry about my being upset. I am not allowed to do any advanced nursing, and we have no war wounded. The Cottage Hospital takes civilian cases only.'

'Even so . . .' her mother sighed. 'I wish your father were still alive so that he might talk to you. You are so very young . . .' She reached over and tucked a strand of Charlotte's blonde hair behind her ear. '. . . and so very determined. You were always such a gentle child, and yet when we discuss this subject I cannot persuade you to change your mind.'

'Because I think it is the right thing to do.' Charlotte spoke urgently. 'The War wasn't over by Christmas last year as people said it might be. We are now in the second summer of fighting and trained nurses will be needed if it lasts another year.'

'Who is talking of war?' said a voice in amusement. 'Not my little sister, pretending to understand politics?'

Charlotte looked up as her brother, sketch-book under his arm, came into the room. 'Stop teasing, Francis,' she said. 'Everyone talks about the War situation. And although I do not read of it as much as you do, I hear enough to know that the Allies are not advancing as quickly as expected.'

'We won at Neuve Chapelle, didn't we?' Mrs Armstrong-Barnes looked at Francis. 'I read that in the newspaper.'

'One has to do more than read the headlines and the official news in order to find out what is going on over there,' said Francis, helping himself to a scone from the tiered cakestand on the table. He took a teacup from his mother. 'We lost a lot of men at Neuve Chapelle. I agree with Charlotte. I think the War will last longer than another year.'

'Well, I only read the interesting bits of the newspaper,' said their mother. 'The part that tells you what is happening here – that is what concerns me. Did you know that your cousin Eugenie has become engaged to Adrian Vermont? He is one of the Vermonts of York, a very well thought of family.' She bit daintily into her cake.

Charlotte stirred her tea briskly. 'Well, good luck to Cousin Eugenie,' she said. 'If it is the same Adrian Vermont I recall meeting at their Midsummer Ball, then she is very welcome to him. His family may be well thought of. I thought he was very spotty and incredibly dull.'

'Charlotte!' cried her mother. 'Don't be vulgar.'

'Actually,' said Francis seriously, 'home news should be the most important part of any newspaper. There is far too much patriotic drum-beating. It is quite wrong.'

'Do you really think it is wrong?' asked Charlotte. She looked across the room to where her brother stood, tall and handsome, with the same blond hair as herself. For all the banter between them she had a great respect for him. Older by almost seven years, he had always been her hero, her protector when the local children had called her names because they lived in such a large house. She greatly valued his opinion.

'Who in their right mind would want to go to war?' said Francis. 'Not the ordinary Prussian or Frenchman, I'll wager. What makes a human being want to kill another who has done him no personal harm? Patriotism. The one thing that can unite people. It takes priority over religious differences, or class, or money, or social position. And then people can be manipulated by others for reasons of power or to gain a few acres of land.' There was a high colour on Francis's cheeks though his face was pale. 'Men and women will die for their country, and unscrupulous leaders use this.'

'Really, Francis,' chided his mother. 'You shouldn't talk like that. It's . . . it's disloyal.'

Francis shrugged and smiled at Charlotte.

'And there you have it,' he said. He stood up. 'It's going to be another fine evening. Care for a walk down to the village before dinner?'

Charlotte jumped up at once.

'Oh yes!' she cried. 'Give me some minutes to change.'

She ran quickly out of the room and up the stairs. Her bedroom looked out over the back of the house to the washing green, the kitchen gardens and the long glass houses by the end wall. She could see the gardener's lad moving between the vegetable rows hoeing the dry earth. Annie the housekeeper came out from the back kitchen with a large wicker washing basket on her hip. She set it down and began unpegging the clothes, the white linen sheets and shirts. Charlotte heard the murmur of their voices. She stood for a few moments by her open window and inhaled the soft fragrant smell of summer.

There was a climbing rose trailing along her window ledge, in full bloom and heavily scented. She pulled a few petals and scattered them in the basin of warm water which Helen, the maid, had left on her night table. It would be good to get out of her starched clothes and away from the smell of disinfectant. When Charlotte had heard that they needed help at the hospital because so many nurses had gone to France she had volunteered at once. Most of her mother's servants were now occupied with war work. Charlotte's own governess had joined the Voluntary Aid Detachment, and to Charlotte this had seemed a more productive way of spending her days than learning housekeeping skills from her mother. Charlotte knew that her mother was unhappy with both her children at the moment. She had expected Charlotte to be a dutiful daughter content to remain at home, and as for Francis . . . Charlotte's brow wrinkled as she thought about her brother who, since he had returned from University, spent his time helping manage the estate or sketching, and steadfastly refused to consider applying for a commission in the Army. Charlotte was aware that Francis was deeply troubled by the conduct of the War, and was at a loss as to how to lift his spirits. He seemed to enjoy being out of doors with his sketch-book, and it had become a custom with them to take a walk each evening before dinner.

Charlotte sponged herself and changed quickly into a day dress, choosing one of finest cotton lawn with a delicate pattern of muted blue flowers which brought up the colour of her grey eyes. The dress draped her slim figure from neck to ankle. She redid her hair, deftly sweeping it up and coiling it on top of her head. Now . . . she looked at herself in the mirror . . . a hat or not? This was an important consideration. Her mother would be faintly scandalized if her daughter walked out hatless. But she was probably resting before dinner and Charlotte would not be subjected to her critical gaze. And it was essential that Charlotte achieve exactly the right effect, for this was not the casual stroll that her mother might imagine it to be. Charlotte knew to the last detail in which direction their walk was going to take them, and precisely whom she was going to encounter. She rummaged through her hatboxes and eventually picked out a straw boater with a blue ribbon round the crown. She set it straight on her head. Mmm . . . too severe. She tilted it back a shade – that was better. Now if she felt a little overdressed she could quickly take it off and swing it idly in her hand.

'Are you ready, little sister?'

Charlotte ran to the window. Francis was standing in the garden below calling up to her.

'Yes,' she called back.

She checked her appearance one more time, pinching her cheeks sharply to give them more colour. Then she skipped happily downstairs.

Francis was helping Annie carry the washing into the house. 'And how are all your children, Annie?' Charlotte heard him ask as he set the basket down.

'Well, Master Francis,' said Annie, handing him the end of a sheet. 'The girls are in service, good houses all six of them, and my two boys, Rory and Ewan, enlisted together a few months ago. The news from the Front had them all fired up. They're training in Shropshire now with a lot of other lads from the village, and desperate to be sent off to where the action is.' She said this last part proudly.

'Let's hope to God that they aren't,' said Francis fervently. He joined the sheet ends and walked towards her, folding it concertina-wise.

'Now, now, Master Francis,' said Annie, 'you've been away at University too long to know what's going on in the world.' She took the folded sheet from him, and, doubling it up once more, placed it on the dresser. 'Our country needs young men, and, thank God, we've got plenty. The Hun wants sorting out, and it's up to Britain to do it.'

As Francis opened his mouth to reply Charlotte interrupted.

'I'm ready,' she said. 'Look,' she did a quick pirouette, 'do you like my dress?'

Annie gazed at her fondly. 'What a lovely young lady you have turned into,' she said. 'I remember when you were just a babe in your carriage. I always said that you'd grow up to be a beauty.'

'Not just a beauty,' added Francis as brother and sister walked arm in arm down the drive, 'but diplomatic too, dear Charlotte. Don't think I didn't notice your timely interruption.'

'Well.' Charlotte laughed and patted his arm. 'I don't think Annie would have appreciated a lecture on the ethics of war. She is obviously very proud to have two sons in uniform.'

They had reached the end of the drive. To the right was the farm road going through a small wood and then into the gentle hills which surrounded their house. To the right lay the village of Stratharden.

'Which way?' asked Charlotte innocently.

Francis turned to her with a gleam in his eye. He patted his sketch-book which was tucked under his arm. 'I want an interesting view to draw. You choose,' he said.

'Umm . . .' said Charlotte, feigning indecision. 'I don't know . . . Didn't you say you wanted a newspaper? There's a shop in the village that is open just now – it would have the evening news.'

'What a good idea!' exclaimed Francis, joining in her play-acting. He took her firmly by the arm. 'Let us go at once and purchase a newspaper.'

Beside him Charlotte gave a little smile and quickened her pace. This evening, quite apart from the business of buying a newspaper, she, Charlotte Mary Armstrong-Barnes, was about to engage in some serious flirting.

Chapter 2

MAGGIE DUNDAS CLIPPED on the lid of the last biscuit tin and took a step back. All the tins lined along behind the shop counter were now closed over for the night. She glanced at the big clock that hung over the front entrance to her father's shop. Nearly closing time, thank goodness! Normally she didn't mind helping out behind the counter, but today she was tired. She was fed up walking back and forth weighing this and measuring that. The shop was so much busier of late, for despite being warned not to, people were beginning to stockpile non-perishable foodstuffs. Her feet were sore, and her head ached too. Listening to the constant talk of war depressed her. Her mother had been poorly for over a week now, and Maggie knew that after she had finished here she would have to climb the stairs to the house above and prepare the family dinner.

'Our Alex had better have those potatoes peeled and on the boil,' she said to her brother. John Malcolm Dundas was behind the counter making up butter portions and wrapping them in white greaseproof paper.

'I'm sure he will.' John Malcolm grinned at her as he eased the wire cutter through the block of butter he had taken from the barrel. 'He's more afraid of you than our Ma. Lend us a hand here, Maggie, won't you?'

'Deed I won't,' she replied sharply. 'I've done my share here today, and I've got Ma to see to, *and* the dinner, while you and Dad will no doubt come upstairs, sit in the easy chairs, read the newspapers and talk politics.'

'We're awfully cross tonight, aren't we?' her brother teased. 'You'll be rushing off to join the Suffragettes if we don't keep our eye on you.'

'And why not?' Maggie faced him, hands on hips. 'Do you think it is fair and right that a woman is not treated equal to a man in this society today? Let me remind you that we are twins and Ma assures me that I was born first, and as such am older than you.'

'What's this! What's this!' Their father had come from the back shop, drawn by the noise of the argument. 'You will disturb your mother. You are always sparring, you two, you're worse than young Alex. Can't you keep the peace for more than two minutes?' He looked from one to the other in annoyance. They were so alike, he thought, and that was the trouble – alike to look at with curly chestnut hair and eyes to match, and alike in temperament, quick to row, but fortunately also quick to forgive.

Maggie was already laughing. 'Sorry, Dad.' She came over and kissed him.

'What are you arguing about?' he asked, softening.

'She's going to join Mrs Pankhurst and break the windows of public buildings,' her twin declared mischievously.

'I'll break that butter pat over your head if you're not careful,' said Maggie. 'Will I close up now, Dad?'

'Aye, just see if thon wee boy's about first.'

Maggie crossed towards the door as her father got an old box and began to put some cracked eggs and bruised fruit in it. She went first to the window and glanced up and down the street, looking for the boy they only knew as 'Willie'. He was one of a large family from the poorer end of the village, where the houses were unsanitary and children played barefoot on earthen streets.

The main street of the village was quiet. Most people were at home having their evening meal. She waved across to Mrs Brunowski, the Polish lady who kept the ladies' outfitters on the opposite side of the street, then she leaned into the window and drew down their own dark blue blind. As she did so she caught sight of two figures sauntering arm in arm towards their shop. Her lip tightened. Miss High-and-Mighty from the big house, and who was that with her? It must be the dreamy brother, freshly returned from University and full of new ideas, she'd heard, to tell others what to do, that had enough to do. And as for herself, Miss Charlotte, cycling up and down to the little cottage hospital every other day, playing at being a nurse. Well, she, Maggie, knew fine well what she was up to, calling in at the shop as often as she could for some trifling message. Making big calf eyes at her brother, and him so gullible he was lapping it up, like a cat at a saucerful of warm milk.

By the time she reached the shop door and began to close over the first half, Maggie had worked herself into a thoroughly bad mood.

'Are we too late?' enquired a pleasant voice at her elbow.

Maggie stopped struggling with the bolt and looked up into the handsome face of Charlotte's brother Francis.

'We only wish to purchase a newspaper,' he added with a charming smile.

'That's all right, I suppose,' Maggie replied grudgingly. She knew that it wouldn't do to offend them. Stratharden House always had a large weekly order delivered, besides which, some of the members of her family might actually welcome their company. She nodded and led the way into the shop.

'Sorry to delay you,' Francis said apologetically to Maggie's dad. 'I just wondered if you had a copy of the evening newspaper?'

'No bother, no bother at all,' said Mr Dundas quickly. 'I've the *Chronicle* here.' He handed Francis the newspaper. 'You'll be wanting to read the war news, I suppose?'

'Not *wanting* to exactly,' said Francis, 'but I suppose one should be aware of what is happening.'

'Oh yes,' agreed Mr Dundas, 'we need to keep up with the news. Now that your University days are over you'll want to be part of it. John Malcolm can't wait for his eighteenth birthday so that he can go off and do his bit.'

Francis said nothing in reply. His sister had wandered across to the opposite counter and was intently examining the display case which held hair ribbons and lace handkerchiefs.

'Can I help you?'

John Malcolm appeared at her side. She gazed at him with clear grey eyes which were on a level with his own.

'I don't know . . .' Charlotte hesitated. 'My mother's birthday is quite soon. It is so difficult to choose a gift for an older person, don't you think?'

John Malcolm nodded vigorously in agreement.

Had Charlotte said that the moon was made of green cheese her brother would have agreed, Maggie thought sourly. She was suddenly conscious of her plain brown dress covered with her shop apron, and her hair not quite in place after a day's work. 'I'll help the lady, John Malcolm,' she said briskly. 'After all, you are busy pricing the butter, aren't you?' she added sweetly.

'Oh, don't trouble yourself. I'll come another day,' said Charlotte. 'You are almost closed and my brother has his newspaper now.' She smiled and managed to meet eyes once again with John Malcolm, before she rejoined her brother. Mr Dundas covered the awkward pause in their conversation.

'Are you still interested in drawing?' He nodded to the sketch-pad under Francis's arm. 'I remember you as a wee lad, you always had a pencil in your fist.'

'I haven't had much time over the last months, but I'm hoping to take it up again more seriously.'

John Malcolm had taken off his apron. 'Let me take our order for tomorrow's milk up to the farm, Dad,' he volunteered.

'Right, son, fine. The slip is on my desk,' said his father, taken aback by this sudden volunteering by one of his children to run an errand.

Francis and Charlotte left the shop. Maggie watched them go from the doorway. A few moments later her brother made to leave.

'Don't break your neck trying to catch them up,' said Maggie as he went past her. 'And I'm serving dinner in twenty minutes, with or without you.'

Her brother turned and walked away from her backwards, grimacing and pulling the most dreadful faces until she eventually had to laugh.

Maggie shook her head. Her emotions were confused. Why should her brother not speak to Miss Charlotte Armstrong-Barnes? Over the last few months he had become quite taken up with this young lady. Was she so possessive of her twin that she did not want him to be fond of anyone else? Or was it this particular person she resented, and why? Had it anything to do with the girl's wealth and position? If she, Maggie, protested equality for her sex, then it should be equality in everything, and both ways, up and down the social scale, shouldn't it?

'Any spoiled goods, miss?' pleaded a small voice beside her.

The ragamuffin child had detached himself from the side of the wall next to the shop and was standing before her.

'Go inside,' said Maggie kindly, 'my dad may have something for you.'

It was hard to tell what age he was, with spindly arms and legs sticking out of outgrown clothes, his thin peaked face still pasty-white despite the long hot summer days. Maggie watched him run away up the street with his box clutched tightly before him. Where was his equality? she wondered.

Chapter 3

JOHN MALCOLM CAUGHT up with Charlotte and Francis on the bridge at the edge of the village.

'Look at the water,' said Francis, leaning out over the bridge. 'How pure and clear it is.'

'And the sound it makes,' said Charlotte, 'so pretty. It seems to be beckoning you. Don't you think so?' She turned to John Malcolm.

'Beckoning you to do what?' he asked.

'Why, to let it run through your fingers, or paddle in the water as we used to do when we were children. Remember the summers when I was little?' she asked her brother. 'We used to walk into the hills with a picnic basket and find a stream to dam and then sail paper boats.'

Francis had opened up his sketch-pad and was making deft strokes with his pencil.

'Why don't we do it again?' cried Charlotte. 'I have a wonderful idea. We could all go on a picnic on the next Bank Holiday.'

'I don't know if I am up to tramping for miles and miles,' said Francis, laughing.

'You could ask Mother if we may take the car out and drive to one of the little lochs, and John Malcolm and his sister could come, and his younger brother too. I'm sure he would like that.'

John Malcolm could imagine only too well how much Alex would like that. Driving around the country in a real motor carriage. 'I'll have to square that away with my father first,' he said. 'The shop has been very busy lately, and we always have lots of work to catch up with on holiday weekends.'

'And you will have to speak to Mother,' said Francis. 'I'm not sure that she will approve of you gallivanting about the countryside.'

Charlotte pulled a face. 'At the moment Mother does not approve of anything I do.'

'That is probably because your head is like my sister's and full of these new ideas of women's place in society,' said John Malcolm.

They had left the bridge and were starting up the country road.

'I'll sit here for a bit,' Francis called after them. He waved his sketch-book in the air. 'I want to see if I can catch the light on the water. Tell Mother I won't be late for dinner.'

'And what if I did think that women should be the same as men?' demanded Charlotte. 'Exactly what is wrong with that?'

'Do I have to remind you of all the ways that men are superior to women?' said John Malcolm, his eyes teasing.

'Hah!' cried Charlotte. 'That proves that you miss the point. You should not talk of superiority, but of equality.'

She had taken off her hat and was swinging it back and forth in one hand, which left, as John Malcolm was quick to notice, the hand closest to his free. In all the previous weeks when they had spoken to each other they had never once been alone together. They turned the bend into the stretch of road which took them out of sight of the village but not yet in view of Charlotte's house. He moved closer, chewed his lip. 'Would you mind if I took your hand?'

For a horrible moment she didn't say anything at all. Then still remaining silent she held out her hand. They walked in silence for a minute or two, he hardly closing his fingers around the hand that rested lightly in his. Now he couldn't think of a thing to say to her. Usually words went flying off his tongue.

She spoke first. 'You were about to tell me,' she said, 'exactly how you were superior to me.'

He looked into her calm grey eyes, and was lost for ever.

'I may have changed my mind,' he said hoarsely.

'Actually,' said Charlotte, 'I do remember an occasion when you were superior. It was one day in the village school. You were in some class above, and much too grand to be bothered with the likes of me. But my ball went on the school roof and I was standing by the railings crying, and you climbed all the way up and threw it down to me. I thought you were wonderful.'

'Really?' he said. 'I suppose I must have been pretty wonderful to climb up on the roof at that age.' He gave her a sidelong look. 'Do you still think I'm wonderful?'

'Oh, I didn't think you were wonderful for more than two minutes,' she replied. 'You asked me my name, and when I told you, you said, "Well that's a mouthful, I think I'll just call you Charlie," and you did.'

' "Charlie",' repeated John Malcolm. 'You must have thought me a terribly rude little boy.'

'Secretly I rather liked it,' said Charlotte.

John Malcolm looked at her. 'In one way it sort of suits you. Would you be offended if I called you Charlie now?'

'As long as you promise never to say it in front of Mother. She might faint away completely if she heard it.'

'Charlie,' said John Malcolm softly. He drew nearer to her as they walked on. 'That will be my special name for you.'

'You will let me know about the picnic?' asked Charlotte as he took his leave of her at the end of her drive.

‘I’ll give a note to Archie, the delivery boy, with your weekly order on Friday,’ said John Malcolm.

‘And you’ll ask your sister? I would so enjoy her company,’ Charlotte added anxiously. ‘It’s just that . . . I’m afraid if she doesn’t accompany us then I will be unable to go.’

‘Oh, Maggie will come all right,’ said John Malcolm confidently as he waved Charlotte goodbye.

But as he returned home he had misgivings which proved to be correct.

‘I don’t have time to go on motoring trips,’ his sister said crossly.

‘Maggie, please,’ he begged her again.

Maggie was standing at the sink in the scullery crashing the dinner plates together in annoyance. ‘No,’ she repeated, reaching past him for the potato pot. ‘I have far too much to do.’

‘I’ll help you,’ he said desperately. He lifted the pan scourer, and grasping the pot began to scrub it furiously.

Maggie regarded him, hands on hips. ‘There’s a first for everything.’

‘Dad said we could have the day off, and you could do with a rest,’ said John Malcolm.

‘All the beds need changed, and Ma is not up to it,’ said Maggie firmly.

'You would enjoy it,' said her brother, 'and Charlotte particularly asked for you to come.'

'She doesn't want my company,' his sister snapped back. 'She wants *your* company, and you're such a gull that you don't see it.'

Her brother did not answer for a moment. Then he said:

'Perhaps I *do* see it, Maggie. Perhaps I want to spend some time with her. Her mother is very indulgent of her, but she might not be allowed to go unless there is another lady in the party.' He slumped sadly against the wall. 'I really like her an awful lot, Maggie.'

Maggie looked at her brother's crestfallen face and her good nature won through.

'All right then,' she said, and was grabbed and kissed all over the top of her head before she had the words out of her mouth.

Chapter 4

THIS MIGHT BE the best day of the whole summer, Charlotte thought, as she awoke on the last Monday of August. She had left her window open the previous evening and as she lay in bed now she could smell and hear the world coming awake. She stretched her arms right up over her head. She was alive, she was nearly sixteen years old, and this was the morning of her picnic. Just for today, she would try to forget there was a war on.

Charlotte quickly got out of bed and looked at the clothes she intended to wear today. Last night the cream dress with the box-pleated skirt had seemed to her simple, yet classically elegant. Matched with a wide-brimmed hat she had thought to be plainly but strikingly dressed. This morning the outfit appeared to her eyes as too ornate and fussy. A little girl playing at dressing up. What would Margaret Dundas wear, she wondered, to suit her dark eyes and hair gleaming with copper highlights? Charlotte thought herself pale and insipid beside her. The older girl was half a head shorter as well, Charlotte remembered, making Charlotte feel tall and ungainly. She decided to wear what she had selected but replaced the heeled shoes with a flatter pair.

Helen, the maid, brought her a cup of tea as she was doing her hair. 'It's a beautiful day for your outing, miss. Here, let me help you with that.' She set the cup and saucer down and fixed some pins in Charlotte's hair.

'What do you think of my dress, Helen?' Charlotte asked her.

'It's lovely. Just perfect for a summer picnic.'

'Not too fussy?' persisted Charlotte.

'Not at all, miss,' said Helen. 'I'd wear that dress to go walking out with my young man any day.'

'And how is Ian?'

'He's just grand, and expects to get leave before he goes off to France. I'm hoping for a winter engagement and a spring wedding.'

Charlotte gasped. 'How can you say that? What makes you think that he'll ask you to marry him?'

Helen laughed. 'Och, there's ways of getting around men. You just make up to them with big eyes and act as though you thought they were the most important creature on earth. Then take a huff but don't tell them what for and they'll start bringing you pretty gifts and try to coax you out of it. And soon you've got them so that they don't know if they're coming or going. I can't believe that you don't know how to play that game. You've got Master Francis wound round your little finger. How else would you have got him to take you on this outing?'

Charlotte laughed right out loud at this. It was true of course. Francis had smoothed away her mother's doubts.

'I don't know . . .' Charlotte's mother had sighed only last night. 'This Dundas family . . . shopkeepers, aren't they? Do you think that they are entirely suitable company, Francis?'

'The Dundas family is *very* respectable,' Francis told his mother firmly. 'And there are not the same strict boundaries here as you might find elsewhere.'

'Living in the country makes everything different,' his mother agreed. 'I might have sent you elsewhere to be educated, but your father always insisted that the village school was as good as any other for elementary education.'

'And indeed it was, Mother,' said Francis. 'Anyway you couldn't have borne us to be away from you when we were little. Look how upset you were even when I was older and went off to school and University.'

'That is certainly true,' she agreed, 'and you were always your father's pet, Charlotte, so he would not part with you. It was he who decided that it would be the village school and private tutoring later.'

Charlotte could hardly remember her father. He had died when she was quite young, but he had been well liked and respected in the area. Francis had told her that their father had held quite radical views about society which their mother did not altogether share.

Her mother still demurred. 'I don't know . . . Charlotte is almost of marriageable age. It is important that she meets the right type of persons.'

'Father would have said that honesty makes the man,' said Francis seriously. 'And Mr and Mrs Dundas are well known for being upright and generous to those less fortunate. Charlotte will be with me and she will be perfectly safe.' He paused. 'Why don't you come along with us if you are so anxious?'

Charlotte gave her brother a look of alarm. He winked at her. She held her breath and did not dare meet her mother's gaze.

'Mmmmm . . . no. I don't think so, dear. It would be too tiring for me in the heat of the day.'

'Then we will say goodnight, as we want an early start tomorrow,' said Francis, and he ushered Charlotte from the room.

Now she dressed quickly and went downstairs and found him calmly eating bacon and eggs. She picked up a piece of toast. 'Are you going to eat all of that?' she asked him. 'You will be ages and we mustn't be late.'

'We won't be late,' said her brother. 'You help Annie with the picnic basket, and I'll bring the car round.'

Charlotte fixed her hat firmly on her head as they set off down the road towards Stratharden. 'Will you let me drive a little today?' she asked. Sometimes when they were out of sight of the house Francis would show her how the gears worked and let her take the wheel.

'You can put your hands on the wheel for two minutes,' he said, 'until we reach the bridge.'

They drew a great deal of interest as they came to a stop in front of the Dundas store. Mrs Brunowski, her children clutching at her skirts, walked over from her shop on the other side of the street to admire the car. Then the Dundas family appeared, including Mrs Dundas who rarely ventured out of doors. A crowd of small boys, among them Willie, the barefoot urchin, stood staring. The men began technical talk, of tyres and treads, and engine horsepower.

'But it'll never actually replace the horse,' declared Mr Dundas.

'Too expensive,' said John Malcolm. 'There was a six-cylinder Siddeley-Deasey advertised in the *Glasgow Herald* last week. A thousand pounds! Who has that amount of money?'

'Only Royalty could afford that,' said Mrs Dundas.

Everyone took a turn to sit in the driver's seat and admire the upholstery.

'It looks very complicated,' said John Malcolm, studying the controls with his brother Alex.

'Not at all,' said Francis. 'Even Charlotte can almost understand it.'

Charlotte pinched his arm. 'Don't be so superior, brother dear. Isn't it time we were off?'

Francis took the hint. 'Ladies in the back, gentlemen in the front,' he declared. 'It will give you some protection from the breeze,' he added as he handed the two girls into the car.

As Margaret Dundas stepped onto the running board and then settled herself down, Charlotte was pleased to note that she was wearing a blue box-pleated dress not dissimilar to her own. Maggie, who had decided for her brother's sake to take part in this with good grace, bestowed on Charlotte a determined smile. Charlotte smiled happily back.

John Malcolm put their picnic basket, a rug and a parasol in the stowage space behind. The small group waved them off.

As they passed through the village, Alex was allowed to honk the horn loudly, despite the fact that the only object in the way was a grey and white cat leisurely crossing the street.

Chapter 5

FRANCIS TOOK THE road into the hills and soon the pastureland dropped away behind them. As the car climbed higher they could see forest and loch below them and wild moorland above.

Charlotte leaned forward and tapped her brother on the shoulder. 'Do you think you could capture this on canvas?' she shouted above the noise of the engine. It was quite beautiful, thought Charlotte, and real. Not a painting, nor a photograph, nor one of the pretty picture postcards that people sent to each other nowadays, but a living landscape that she could see and smell. The trouble in Europe had prevented Charlotte from taking her promised Cultural Tour abroad, and she longed to see all the things Francis had seen at her age. He had told her of the sculptures in Greece, the buildings in Italy, and the paintings in France which reflected the grandeur of nature and inspired his own work. But she was able to experience some of that glory right here, thought Charlotte, looking around her. She felt elated merely by being young and alive among such beauty and promise.

They stopped in the hills by the side of the road and unpacked the baskets.

'Across that stile, I think,' said Francis, 'and if we follow the path we should come to a small river.'

They set out their picnic by the edge of the water, spreading the rugs under a large tree. John Malcolm tied twine round the bottles of ale and lemonade and sank them in the water to cool them. Alex had brought some sailboats that his father had made and they all tried, without much success, to sail them on the water.

Charlotte gave up first. 'It's far too hot,' she said. 'I'm going to sit in the shade under the tree.'

Not very long after she was joined by John Malcolm. He took off his jacket and stretched out beside her on the grass. 'I didn't want you to be lonely off here all by yourself,' he said. 'I thought I'd come and join you.'

'Oh, don't spoil your game on my account,' said Charlotte. 'I'm quite happy here on my own.'

'So . . .' he looked at her carefully, 'you'd rather I went away again?'

She twirled her parasol and studied him from under her lashes. 'I didn't say that,' she replied softly.

He rolled over onto his stomach so that he was gazing up at her. In her cream dress with the dappled light of the green leaves behind her he thought she was the most beautiful thing he had ever seen. He looked down at the grass and then up at her again. 'Shall I make you a daisy chain?'

She folded her parasol and put it aside. 'I haven't seen a daisy chain for such a long time. Can you really make one?'

'Easiest thing in the world.'

They were both soon laughing at his clumsy attempts to slot the slender stems together. Eventually Charlotte took it from him and they sat side by side, heads close together, while she showed him how to do it.

He is very handsome, she thought, as she stole little glances at him from time to time. His face was set in concentration as he followed her instructions, the strong tanned fingers among the fragile petals.

'There!' he said at last. 'Now, how do you join both ends together?'

'Ah, that is the tricky part . . .' said Charlotte. She put her fingers over his and gently drew the last stem opening over the first flower head.

There was a long pause. They could hear shouts of laughter from the riverbank but they seemed far away.

He caressed her fingers gently. 'You seem so delicate . . . and serene, and . . . and . . . I don't know . . . good.' He raised her fingers to his lips.

Charlotte's heart was like a caged bird, her mind was in confusion. This was more than flirting, she must be falling in love. How fortunate she was that her feelings for John Malcolm seemed to be returned by him. He took the daisy chain and wound it round her wrist.

They both looked towards the water as the shouts of laughter grew louder. Maggie's boat was sinking and its line was trailing in the water out of reach. Francis had taken off his socks and shoes and, having rolled up his trouser legs, was gallantly wading out to rescue it.

'Is it very strange having a sister as a twin?' asked Charlotte.

'Maggie's a good sort. She works very hard, in the shop and looking after the house,' said John Malcolm. 'We argue a lot, but she's a great pal.'

Charlotte thought about her and Francis. They were close, too, but in a different way. He looked out for her as his little sister, but she didn't really have a friend, a 'pal' to use John Malcolm's word.

Francis had reached the boat and was now holding it triumphantly above his head. Maggie cheered and clapped loudly. Alex had taken his boots and socks off and had joined Francis in the water. John Malcolm scrambled to his feet.

'My mother will have fourteen fits if he falls in,' he told Charlotte. 'They were both very ill when he was born, and she still worries about him a lot.' He ran down to the water's edge.

Charlotte leaned her back against the tree and watched the rescue attempt as John Malcolm called to his young brother to come ashore. Maggie came to join her and together they unwrapped the sandwiches of cold meat, tomato and egg. Charlotte chatted easily as they set out the napkins and the cutlery.

It's shining out of her, Maggie thought as she helped put out the food: cheese and pickles, baps and buttered scones, fruit and apple pie. She had noticed the two heads close together earlier; her brother's dark curls a foil for the girl's soft blonde hair. She tried to put her feelings of annoyance aside. Why should they not be happy together? An awful thought occurred to her. Was this jealousy she was feeling?

John Malcolm, now barefoot, was capering about in the water with Francis and Alex. Eventually he grabbed Alex and swung him across his shoulders and marched towards them. He was laughing as he tumbled his brother down onto the grass beside them.

'One bag of coal delivered.'

Maggie laughed too, then. Surrounded by their happiness she could not help herself.

The boys dried off in the sun as they ate their picnic, and it was Alex who heard it first. He had wandered back down to skim stones across the water, while Francis sketched and they all talked of what they might do in an ideal world.

They got to their feet when they heard Alex shouting. He was pointing to the sky and jumping up and down.

'What is it?' asked Maggie, shading her eyes and squinting at the sun.

The noise, at first an indistinct buzzing, rapidly became louder until both earth and sky were filled with an almighty roaring. The two girls clapped their hands over their ears.

'It's a flying machine!' yelled Alex. He was waving and yelling at the top of his voice.

The pilot must have caught sight of them and took the chance to show off. He banked, turned and flew back over their heads. His face was hidden by helmet and goggles but they could see him wave to them quite clearly. Then, gaining height, he did a graceful loop the loop, waggled his wings and was gone.

The sky was empty and quiet. Alex could hardly contain himself.

'That's what I'm going to be when I am older, a flyer.'

'I wouldn't tell our ma that just yet,' advised Maggie. 'Anyway it's probably one of those inventions that'll come to nothing. It doesn't look safe to me, all cardboard and bits of string.'

'I don't know . . .' said Francis. He closed over his sketchbook. 'I've been to an air show at Hendon in England, and they are developing all the time.' He sighed. 'I suppose being at war pushes the need for improvements forward.'

'Oh yes!' cried Alex enthusiastically. 'I could have a great big aeroplane and put lots of bombs in it, and then fly over the enemy and drop the bombs on top of them. I hope the War isn't over by the time I grow up.'

Charlotte looked anxiously at Francis. She hoped he wouldn't say anything out of place. Alex was still a boy, barely fourteen at most, excited at seeing an aeroplane.

'I'm tired of sitting still for so long,' she said quickly. 'I brought racquets and a ball. Shall we play a game?'

They returned home just as twilight was falling. The headlamps of the car cut a bright beam across the road, and although Alex honked the horn at every corner the only traffic they met was a herd of cows sauntering lazily along the road. The old herdsman touched his forehead as they passed. Then he shook his head and stood gazing down the dusty road after them.

'Do you realize something?' Charlotte said to Francis as they unpacked the picnic basket in the kitchen. 'We managed to spend a whole day in company and we hardly discussed the War at all.'

That night she slept with a daisy chain under her pillow.

Chapter 6

BUT AS THE days shortened in the weeks that followed it became impossible not to talk about the War. It had now become part of everyday life. Collection tins stood on the counters of all the shops. Churches and schools were used as centres for donations of food, clothing and gifts to send to the men at the Front. Children were encouraged to write letters and send sweets to their soldier friends. Women ripped out old jumpers and gathered the wool to knit scarves, gloves and socks. Charlotte's mother and her friends ran tea afternoons, charging guests one shilling to attend and taking it in turns to entertain. Annie often helped out on these occasions, and enjoyed the idea that she was doing something for her boys. Rory and Ewan were now in France and had written home to say that they expected to be sent forward soon. Mrs Armstrong-Barnes's sister wrote from Belfast with news of her own children. All the girls were involved in some kind of nursing, and her sons, Connor and Phelan, had both obtained commissions and joined their father in the Irish Guards. Nothing had been said openly in the house about Francis's lack of involvement but Charlotte knew that her mother was uncomfortable that he was not serving in any capacity.

The casualty lists grew each day, and as they grew, so did the Army's need for more men. Special newspapers and posters were printed and circulated, urging young men to join up. Factories and shops posted leaflets encouraging workers to enlist, and huge billboards shrieked out the message: 'Join up! The safety of our Empire is in your hands!' Newspapers had photographs of Glasgow trams carrying adverts for women conductors, the first city in Britain to do so. In the shop Maggie glanced at these, and wondered at the sudden reversal of public opinion. Previously, it was frowned upon if a woman worked outside the home, and if they did, they were restricted to certain types of occupation. Now, they were being implored to take jobs to release men and enable them to enlist! Wives and girlfriends were told that the safety of their homes and children depended on them sending their men to fight for King and Country. 'Tell them to go!' said one poster. 'When the War is over and your husband or son is asked "What did you do in the Great War?" – is he to hang his head in shame because *you* would not let him go?'

Charlotte was working more days and longer hours at the hospital, so Francis often walked alone to the village in the late afternoon to buy a newspaper. The jingoistic tones of the headlines contrasting with the constant news of death lowered his spirits. He felt helpless in the face of what he saw as some desperate intent by civilization to destroy itself, and absented himself from the house before any visitors were due to arrive, spending long hours in the library, or walking the hills, sketch-book in hand. But there came a day when even he could not avoid what was happening.

The King's Own Scottish Borderers Regiment mounted a big recruiting drive in Central Scotland, and about 200 men from the Reserve Battalion conducted a series of marches throughout the area, lasting several days. Led by a pipe band they marched through Linn, Royalmount and Ferryglen, arriving in Stratharden early one weekday afternoon. They had permission to billet for the night in the field behind the school, and as soon as lessons were finished Alex and the rest of the schoolchildren were swarming all over their camp.

The soldiers were constructing some trenches 'exactly as they would be at the Front', with a real dug-out where the officers sat discussing battle plans. The villagers were invited to walk along the line and keep a lookout over the parapet 'just as the soldiers do' by using a box-periscope.

Alex did not join in as the younger children ran up and down the lines and played football with the off-duty soldiers. He had something more important in mind. Approaching the most senior Private he said, 'My name is Alexander Dundas, and I'd like to know as much as you can tell me about the Army because I'm going to be a soldier when I'm old enough if the War is not over.' He squinted up at the tall Private whose bulk almost blotted out the sun. 'Do you think it will be? Over soon? The War, I mean?'

The Private looked down at the earnest face of the boy before him. Then he drew himself up and gave Alex a full formal salute. 'I'm Senior Private Cooper,' he said, 'and I'm heartily glad you're going to be a soldier, because, pal, we need all the help we can get. But even if the War is over by the time you're old enough, soldiering is still a grand life.' He took off his helmet and put it on Alex's head. 'Now . . .' He held up what looked like an odd-shaped spade. 'This is called an entrenching tool. Would you like to learn how to use it, and help me dig a bit of a trench?'

A Recruiting Office had been set up in the school assembly hall, and later that evening, after he had had his tea, Alex went back along there. The pipe band was drumming up in the playground, and the soldiers were executing various parade manoeuvres. The noise of the music and the presence of the soldiers had attracted quite a crowd from the whole locality, including a sprinkling of young ladies. Already a number of men were waiting to give their names and addresses. Onlookers applauded as they went inside, one by one.

Alex waited patiently. After about ten minutes the soldier on duty at the door turned away to answer an enquiry. Alex seized his chance and slipped inside. Private Cooper was sitting behind a table in front of the stage with the recruiting sergeant.

Alex went up to him and saluted. 'Need any help, sir?'

'At ease, soldier,' said Private Cooper. He turned to his sergeant. 'What do you reckon, sir? This man is reporting for duty. Acquitted himself well on trench work earlier.'

The Sergeant inspected Alex thoroughly. Then he leaned across the table so that his face was on a level with Alex's own. 'One of the most important jobs at the Front is the Company Runner. He's up and down the line through shot and shell, bringing ammunition to the men, messages to the officers, rations to everyone. He has to be nimble, clever, fearless, and . . .' the Sergeant winked broadly, 'able to nose out supplies where folks will tell him there are none.' He turned to Private Cooper. 'I'd say if your soldier could scout us out two mugs of mother's brew, *with* sugar, mind, then he'd be up for a decoration.'

Alex saluted and ran off down the corridor. It required some undercover work in the teachers' staff room, but he was back in ten minutes with two mugs of well-sugared tea.

The Sergeant broke off from his form-filling to take a huge mouthful. He smacked his lips and wiped the back of his mouth with his hand. 'If we had more lads like that in France, this war would be done in half the time.'

Alex thought he would burst with pride. For the next hour, while the makeshift recruiting office was open, he stood to attention behind the two soldiers ready for further orders. And he watched closely everything that went on.

It was almost time to pack up when a hired hand from one of the outlying farms came in. Alex knew him. He was only a year older than Alex himself, and had finished his schooling that summer.

He came up to the table and gave his name.

The Sergeant looked at him keenly. 'Date of birth?' he said, and as the boy hesitated, he asked, 'How old are you?'

'Nineteen,' the boy lied.

'Sorry, son.' The Recruiting Sergeant grinned at him and shook his head. 'The Army has had too many complaints from mothers wanting their under-age boys back. I'll need your birth certificate.' As the boy went away, the Sergeant turned to the Senior Private who was helping him and said in a low voice, 'If it'd been in the city we might have got away with it, but not out here where everybody knows everybody's business before it happens.'

The Private laughed. 'You're right there, Sarge. His ma would be chasing after the parade tomorrow, and it would be her fist not a flag she'd be waving at you.'

'How did the Sergeant know that last boy was too young?' Alex asked Private Cooper as he helped him carry his things back to his tent in the field.

'He was awfie small, and didn't know his date of birth. And he never looked the Sarge right in the eye when he told him how old he was.'

'There's lots of small men,' said Alex. 'Supposing you are small and the right age, can't you join up?'

'Och aye,' said the Private. 'Some of the big cities like Glasgow and Liverpool have Bantam Battalions. They're for the little 'uns, and right fearsome fighters they are too.'

'Bantam Battalions.' Alex repeated the phrase in his head so that he would not forget it.

'I think you deserve something for being on duty so long,' said Private Cooper. He gave Alex a haversack and put some small round tins in it. 'Maconochie rations, pork and beans, they're what we use on active service.'

Happily Alex went off home. He would ask Maggie to cook this for dinner, and then he could taste what real soldiers ate when they were in battle.

In Stratharden House, preparations were being made for dinner. Mrs Armstrong-Barnes had invited the staff officers, Captain Dudley and his second lieutenant, to dinner that evening. Charlotte and her mother were fussing over the table settings when Francis came into the dining room.

'I beg to be excused dinner this evening,' he said.

His mother frowned. 'That is not possible, Francis. We have a duty of hospitality and you are the man of the house.'

'But not quite the right sort of man for this evening, surely,' Francis said mockingly. 'I am not in uniform, and I appreciate that it is an acute embarrassment to you that I have declined to join Kitchener's boys. I ask that you entertain His Majesty's glorious forces without me.'

Charlotte saw her mother's colour rise.

'Your sarcasm is inappropriate,' said Mrs Armstrong-Barnes coldly. 'These men have recently returned from France, and are recovering from various wounds. No matter what your personal opinions are, one should respect their commitment and have compassion for what they have suffered. Also,' she added, 'you are my son. In the absence of my husband I expect your support.'

Francis's smile faded, then he said in a low voice, 'Forgive my flippancy. I will attend dinner this evening.'

Charlotte glanced anxiously from her mother to her brother. She hated friction between friends or family.

'Don't look so worried, little sister,' said Francis. 'I'll be on my best behaviour.'

Much to Charlotte's relief Francis kept his promise. When Captain Dudley, accompanied by a second lieutenant of about twenty years old, arrived just after eight o'clock he was there to greet them. During dinner he asked interested and informed questions about the progress of the War. Both officers had seen action at Neuve Chapelle. At one point, when the Captain spoke of 'unavoidable slaughter' Charlotte saw Francis's lips tighten, but her brother did not make any comment on this, and only said he hoped things would progress better with the Autumn Offensive.

'I suppose the idea is to sustain a breakthrough along a cohesive section?'

'You are remarkably well informed,' said Captain Dudley. 'Obviously you are taking a keen interest. I hope that your commission comes through soon.'

There was the slightest of pauses.

'More wine?' said Francis.

'Charlotte is doing her bit too,' said Mrs Armstrong-Barnes smoothly. 'She nurses at the Cottage Hospital.'

'I would hardly call it proper nursing,' said Charlotte. 'I am one of the Voluntary Aid Detachment, although I am taking Nursing Certificates. We have not dealt directly with any wounded soldiers. The Cottage Hospital does now take every civilian case possible so that it can free up space elsewhere, but I do little more than basic first aid . . . and interminable bandage-rolling.'

'My dear,' said Captain Dudley. 'You have no idea how the sisters and orderlies are valued by the men at the Front. They are truly magnificent, and work under the most appalling conditions. I have quite reversed my opinion of the fairer sex. They can be as stout-hearted as any man.'

The young Lieutenant, who had not taken his eyes from Charlotte's face all evening, nodded his agreement. 'Without them I surely would have died. When one is wounded, the sight of a nurse is like a vision of heaven.'

Charlotte laughed. 'You would change your mind if you saw what I wear when on duty. The uniform is very heavily starched and quite unbecoming.'

'I think you would look attractive no matter what you were wearing,' the young Lieutenant said sincerely.

Charlotte lowered her eyes.

'Well, you had that poor Second Lieutenant well and truly trussed like a turkey,' Francis said to Charlotte after the two officers had departed.

'Whatever do you mean?' asked Charlotte.

'I think what Francis means,' said Charlotte's mother, smiling, 'is that you have an admirer.'

'An admirer!' exclaimed Charlotte, blushing.

Francis grabbed his sister round the waist. 'Look at you,' he said, 'turning all pink and feminine. You're growing up so fast, little sister. I think our tree-climbing days are over.'

'You left those days behind long before me,' said Charlotte, pushing her brother away from her.

'More's the pity.'

'We can't remain children for ever, Francis,' said Charlotte gently.

'Yes, but I'd like the children to have their childhood at least,' said Francis. He turned away to go upstairs to bed, disinclined to explain further what he meant. Earlier, from a hill above the village he had seen the schoolchildren playing with the soldiers. They were fascinated of course with the excitement of it all. The band played stirring tunes, and soldiers mingled with them on the streets of their little village, hat badges and buttons glinting. Had it been peacetime, it would not have affected him so much, but watching, and knowing the purpose of the Army's visit, had made Francis incredibly sad. He turned at the top of the staircase and called down to Charlotte:

'I hope that you go tomorrow, and wave him off, otherwise his heart will be broken.'

The whole village had turned out the next morning to see the soldiers leave. School was cancelled and people thronged the pavements with the children in front, lined along the edge, waving flags. The Dundas family stood at the shop door to watch the march-past. The band came first with the pipes playing 'We're no awa tae bide awa', flags streaming out in the wind. Behind them the soldiers marched in four formation, Captain Dudley leading at the front. They were cheered at every street corner. As soon as he could, John Malcolm, closely followed by Alex, slipped away from his parents and sister. He worked his way through the crowds until he was beside Charlotte.

'Isn't it glorious?' he said, eyes shining.

'Glorious,' Alex repeated.

Charlotte looked at Alex. He reminded her so much of herself when younger, tagging along after Francis, copying everything he did and said.

'They need sixty men to get up to full strength. They got fifteen from us,' John Malcolm told Charlotte.

'Better than Linn or Ferryglen,' said Alex proudly. 'Private Cooper told me that there's talk of a big battle soon. They could be in France by the end of the month.'

'I so wish I was going now, with the rest of the lads,' said John Malcolm. 'It's so frustrating to be left at home and not be part of it all.'

Chapter 7

AT THE HOSPITAL the next day Charlotte kept thinking about her conversation with John Malcolm as she went about her work. She understood his feelings. Her own motivation in offering to help at the hospital had come from a feeling of obligation to assist the war effort, and to be in some way 'part of it all'.

When she had approached the Superintendent of the Cottage Hospital she had been made most welcome. He had been grateful that the daughter of Mrs Armstrong-Barnes had chosen their humble little hospital to do her voluntary work. In addition to having an extra pair of hands he saw that it could be socially and financially to their advantage. Charlotte had suspected that her mother's position and wealth had smoothed out any objections there might have been to her youth and lack of experience. She had worked hard to prove herself, to let it be seen that she was not put off by disagreeable tasks, and it wasn't long before the rest of the staff realized that she was quite serious in her intent. They let her assist more and more, until she now felt that she was a valued part of the team. For the most part, it was enjoyable. The Matron was kind, and the nurses and sisters patient in instructing her, to the extent that she was now training to do some genuine nursing. They were pleasant company, and she was heartily glad that she had an excuse not to take part in the social round that her mother had mapped out for her. She realized that she actually looked forward to her days on duty. The menial tasks did not bother her, and she found that she liked helping people. Best of all was when she was allowed to attend to patients, and was rewarded by a thank-you and a smile. Their smiles were always readily returned by her and that became her trademark. One day the Matron called her aside, and said, 'In time, Miss Armstrong-Barnes, you will be a gifted nurse. I have watched you serve with a quiet comforting word, and meet the eyes of the seriously ill with a smile. Not every nurse can do that.'

The feeling of pleasure this gave Charlotte lasted for days. She was intelligent enough to appreciate that she could not have attained the warm feeling of satisfaction without first having done the unpleasant tasks. She was also perceptive enough to know that this situation would not have been arrived at if there had been no war. Without the deaths and killing in Europe she would not be in the hospital at all.

It upset her a little to think this way but she knew that it was true. If the War had not happened, her life would be very different. To pursue any career, even those considered respectable for a woman, such as governess, would have been considered selfish. She did not need money, and therefore it would be quite wrong of her to take a position and deprive those who did. At this moment, without the War, she would be looking to make a good marriage and be learning the skills of managing her own home. She wondered how fulfilling that would have been. Or might she have been happy to accept it as her lot in life, not knowing any different?

These thoughts were in her mind when she came across two nurses, Grace Howells and Emily Earnshaw, talking in the nurses' rest room.

Emily called Charlotte over. 'Grace and I are thinking of volunteering for the Scottish Women's Hospital Group. We want to go out to France,' she said. She waved her hand towards the window. 'Anything to get away from this dull weather.'

Charlotte sat down beside them. She wasn't fooled by Emily's joke about the weather. Underneath the offhand manner was a woman who thought carefully before making decisions. Emily was the one who read out the newspaper headlines and kept everyone up to date with what the Red Cross and St John's Ambulance were doing.

'They say that a lot of men die through lack of immediate attention when wounded,' added Grace. 'It's terrible to think that if only there were a few more nurses then they might live.'

Charlotte knew that Grace wrote each day to her sweetheart and worried desperately about him. 'I know what you mean,' said Charlotte. 'I feel so *useless* stuck here, and it will be even worse when John Malcolm . . .' Her voice tailed off and she blushed. When speaking to her friends she had only ever mentioned John Malcolm Dundas in a very general way, and was unaware that they knew all about her blossoming romance.

'Now that a *certain person,*' Emily winked broadly at Grace, 'will soon be enlisting, Charlotte may find life in Stratharden a bit dull.'

'That's not what I mean,' protested Charlotte, her face now bright red. 'It's just that there seems to be no-one of my age left at home.' She stopped as the truth of the words she had just spoken struck her. There *were* very few young men and women about, and the ones that she saw were mostly in uniform. Her friends and the playmates of her youth were involved. Annie's two sons, the stable boy, the young men Francis brought to visit during his vacations, all had gone to France. And the girls too were busy elsewhere, many nursing or doing other war work. Whole families, of sometimes ten or even twelve children, were caught up in it. 'I feel I ought to be doing more,' Charlotte went on. 'You two will go off to France, and everyone seems to be doing something definitely connected with the War except me.'

'You could apply to one of the city hospitals,' said Grace. 'Or one of the new military ones which have been specially opened to cope with the wounded.'

'There are so many wounded,' said Charlotte. 'One wonders who is left in France.'

'They are not telling us the half of it,' Emily said darkly. 'If you read the latest newspaper reports carefully you can tell that last battle around Loos did not go as well as they said it did.'

This was similar to what Francis was saying, thought Charlotte. The official newspaper reports told of parapets 'melting away' and barbed wire disappearing under the Allied bombardment. Of British and French troops breaking through on a front many miles long. But more recent news seemed to indicate that the Allies had paid dearly for their initial success, and that the price had been a huge number of casualties, that reserve battalions had been used, but they were untrained and had been sent in too late. Stories were passed from mouth to mouth, and the tales told seemed unbelievable. They said that the men sent forward had no clear instructions, and that they carried insufficient firepower to keep their objectives.

Grace shrugged. 'Who knows what to believe? Once we get there, Charlotte, we will write to you and tell you all about it.'

It was not only in the hospital that there were stories being told of the inefficiency of the Allied offensive. One evening in mid-October just before closing time in the shop Maggie asked her father about it.

'People are saying that we had not enough shells to win the battles around Loos. Could that be true?'

Her father glanced beyond her head. Francis had just come into the shop. 'There's a man who might know.' He handed Francis his newspaper. 'You keep a close eye on what is happening, Mr Armstrong-Barnes, what do you think?'

Francis shrugged. 'I know very little more than what is in the newspapers.' He hesitated. 'However . . . it would appear that there is a shortage of ammunition. *The Times* carried a report recently by trade union representatives who visited the Front in September. They reported that there was a need for more shells.'

Maggie's father snorted. 'Trade unions! Agitators, no doubt.'

'Well, you must read the news and interpret it in your own way,' said Francis. 'The article stated that it was the officers in particular who wished it to be known at home that there was an inadequate supply of ammunition.'

'That is appalling,' exclaimed Maggie.

Francis gave her a wry smile. 'I suppose it is. After all, if one gets in a fight, then the very least one can do is ensure that one's gun is bigger than the other fellow's, and that one has at least as many bullets to fire.'

Maggie looked at him. There was something about his tone of voice which suggested that he was not taking the subject seriously.

But it *was* serious, very serious indeed. So serious in fact that after thinking about it for several days she decided that she was going to do something about it herself. One night halfway through dinner she announced her decision.

'They're advertising for munitions workers,' she said, 'and I might apply.' She glanced at her brother across the table, and then said in an innocent voice to no-one in particular, 'Village gossip tells me that Miss Charlotte Armstrong-Barnes from the big house is now taking a Nursing Certificate. If she can do something to help, so can I.' She had the satisfaction of seeing her brother's face colour up.

'You are needed in the shop,' said her father.

'The money I bring in can be used to employ someone in the shop, the boy Willie for example. Goodness knows, with all those children, his mother would appreciate some money coming in.'

'*Your* mother appreciates *your* help,' her father said shortly. 'You know that she keeps poor health.'

Maggie's mother stretched her hand out and pressed Maggie's own. 'I couldn't manage without you,' she said.

'Alex will have to do more,' Maggie said firmly. 'Being the youngest, he's been spoiled by us all. When we were his age John Malcolm and I did many more chores in the house and the shop. Alex is up the glen every night after school, doing goodness knows what.'

'We want him to stay longer at school if he can so he needs time to study at home, and he's barely fourteen,' protested Maggie's mother.

'He's a big lad for his age,' said Maggie. 'And can fetch and carry as well as I can.'

'There's men's work and women's work,' said her father.

'Look at the casualty lists!' Maggie's voice rose. 'If the War goes on like this there will be no men left!'

'I am engaged in war work,' said Alex importantly.

'And so will I be,' said Maggie. 'You can help out a bit more around the house.'

'I do enough,' said Alex.

'More needs to be done,' said Maggie pleasantly.

'Stop bickering. I want to hear no more of this,' said her father.

Maggie glared at her father. She was almost eighteen years old and he had chided her in the same terms as her little brother! He was viewing her discussion as though it were part of a small boy's squabble. If Alex had spoken to John Malcolm in that manner he would have had his ear cuffed. Her twin was due the respect of a man, but, as a woman, she was relegated to the status of a child.

She made a huge effort to control her temper. 'There is a munitions factory at Springbank on the outskirts of Edinburgh. Tomorrow I'm catching the early morning bus there to see if they will take me on.'

Maggie's father gave her a severe look. 'Your mind's being affected by all this women's emancipation nonsense.'

'Actually,' said Maggie, 'I don't read enough about that "nonsense", as you call it.'

'There you are then,' said her father. 'You're not in a position to make decisions about your life. You don't have sufficient knowledge of what is going on in the world.' Maggie's father put down his knife and fork. 'I am not prepared to allow you—' he began, when John Malcolm interrupted.

‘I think it’s a great idea, Maggie. It’s terrible to be stuck here when our friends are fighting their hearts out for us. Everyone should be doing all they can. There isn’t much time left now until I join up, but I’ll help out so that you can go and do war work.’

Maggie’s father looked from one twin to the other, and then he closed his mouth.

In a way her father was right, Maggie thought as she washed up after dinner. She *didn’t* know about the things that the men discussed. Francis had mentioned an article about the lack of munitions. No-one had told her about that, hence her ignorance. She relied on others to tell her what was going on. It suddenly occurred to her how vulnerable that made her. In her situation others could decide what she should know, and more importantly *not* know. What was it Francis Armstrong-Barnes had said earlier in the shop? ‘You must read the news and interpret it in your own way.’ Her father and brother usually read the newspaper after dinner while she cleared up. Then they discussed it with each other while she and her mother knitted or darned and sometimes listened to them talk. Why was that? She could read, as well, if not better, than any of them. Was it because she had much more to do in the evening, or was she unconsciously following her mother's behaviour in deferring intellectual activities and decisions to the males in the house?

Later that evening, when her father and brother had finished with the newspaper, Maggie spread it out on the kitchen table. For the first time in her life she read a newspaper from front page to last.

Francis, on his way home, head down, reading his own newspaper, almost let Charlotte run into him on her bicycle before he noticed her. She dismounted and he pushed the bicycle for her as they walked home together.

'More bad news?' She nodded towards the newspaper he had tossed into the basket at the front of her cycle.

Francis sighed. 'I'm afraid so. Despite trying to return the favour, by *us* trying to gas *them* this time, it looks as though the engagement round Loos has been a costly mess.'

'Matron was told today that we have to double our bed capacity,' said Charlotte. 'We must take more civilian patients. There are so many wounded coming over from France that the hospitals elsewhere cannot cope.'

'How many thousands will it take before this folly is seen for what it is?' asked Francis wearily. He propped Charlotte's cycle by the main door and followed her inside.

Charlotte didn't answer. Annie was standing in the hallway turning a telegram over and over in her hands.

Francis frowned at the stunned expression on the old housekeeper's face. 'Is that telegram for Mother?' he asked. 'Do you want me to take it up to her?'

'No, Master Francis,' said Annie. 'It's for me.' She looked up at him and her face seemed to age as she spoke. 'Would you read it out to me? I don't think I understand what it says.'

Francis took the telegram and read it. He raised his eyes and Charlotte saw his stricken face. 'Annie,' he said gently. 'It's about your boys.'

The older woman's eyes searched his face. 'Yes,' she said dully. 'Ewan and Rory.'

'It says that . . .' Francis cleared his throat, 'that . . . Rory and Ewan are missing, believed killed in action.'

'Why do they say "*believed* killed"?' said Annie. 'Don't they know if they have been killed or not? That's the bit I don't understand.'

Charlotte stared at Annie and then her gaze went back to Francis. Her mind tried to close around and comprehend what she had just heard. Rory and Ewan, Annie's two boys who had taught both Francis and her how to ride and fish, could now be dead.

'Tea, I think,' said Francis. He took Annie by the arm. 'Let's go down to the kitchen and sit for a bit.'

Charlotte made tea while Francis settled Annie in a chair. He sat down beside her.

'Charlotte will fetch Mother in a minute. We have a cousin who is a major; he might be able to find out a bit more. You wouldn't, by any chance, know where they were stationed?'

'They're not supposed to say,' said Annie, 'but some of the lads write home using codes, and Helen's brothers told her the name of the place. It is somewhere in Belgium – near a place called Loos.'

Charlotte brought the tea to the table. She saw that Francis was avoiding her gaze.

'It says "missing",' Annie repeated again. 'It doesn't say that they've actually been killed, does it?'

'It doesn't,' Francis said, 'but . . .'

Charlotte looked at her brother desperately. He caught her eye, and did not continue. Charlotte noticed his hand shake as he lifted the teapot.

1916

Chapter 8

AT THE END of the village, on a cold grey day in January 1916, Charlotte got on the morning bus to Edinburgh. She was due to begin work today at Springbank Military Hospital for three days a week as a nursing assistant. It was an appointment secured for her by the Matron at the Cottage Hospital who had written a strong letter of recommendation.

'They will take you, though they think you very young,' she had told Charlotte, 'and part of me agrees with them.' As Charlotte opened her mouth to protest, the Matron raised her hand and continued, 'I know that you will soon be sixteen, but we have protected you somewhat here, and you will not find that in a bigger, busier hospital.' She frowned, and gave Charlotte a slightly worried look. 'Indeed the opposite might be the case. All I can say is good luck, and if you want to return I will be happy to see you.'

Despite the bleak January weather Charlotte had been almost glad when Christmas and New Year were over and she could begin real war work in the hospital in the city. It had been such a dreary time compared with previous winter holidays Charlotte had known. Her memories of the Christmases when she was small were of days crisp with excitement. Going with Francis and the gardener on Christmas Eve to pick out a tree. Walking beside the donkey cart, her hand on the bridle. The crackle of the frosty earth beneath the wheels, the little donkey's breath puffing in the cold air. Running home ahead through the gathering gloom with the house all lit up at the top of the drive. Baking gingerbread biscuits with Annie, and hanging them on the tree with the paper decorations and striped candy sugar canes.

Now everything had changed. Their summer picnic seemed an age ago, and Christmas would never be the same again. Her birthday came in early January, and Charlotte was acutely aware that it was not just she who had altered. The end of 1915 and the beginning of 1916 marked a distinct shift in attitudes and manners of the people she knew.

John Malcolm had celebrated his eighteenth birthday in November, and he and Eddie Kane had enlisted at once in the King's Own Scottish Borderers. His training was completed and he was now wildly eager to be away, and talked about the War with a reckless enthusiasm which infected Alex and frightened Charlotte a little. Nevertheless, her first sight of him in uniform had caused her heart to quicken within her. She was terribly proud of him, and felt some sort of reflected glory when she found out that he had recently been promoted to lance-corporal.

In Stratharden House itself there was an uneasy quietness. Charlotte was more sympathetic than her mother to Francis's anti-war stance. She knew her brother to be a thoughtful person and believed that he would have considered all aspects carefully before adopting this position. But there was now a definite tension among the remaining members of the household. Helen was in a constant state of worry about Ian, her young man, and although Annie, the housekeeper, went about her work cheerfully enough, she didn't sing as she used to. She no longer joked with the delivery boys, and only smiled if someone smiled at her first. Mrs Armstrong-Barnes realized that she was no longer able to communicate fully with either of her children. She worried that Charlotte, on her regular walks to the village with Francis, was perhaps seeing a little too much of John Malcolm Dundas, but she could remember being young herself and, as Francis had pointed out, the young man wasn't entirely unsuitable. As for her son, she found it most difficult now to have a conversation with him. She suspected that he busied himself with estate business to avoid her company, indeed any company. She felt that her children had entered adulthood without her, and that the world was moving too swiftly for her to cope with. Christmas had been strained, with news of Allied setbacks and a great number of casualties.

Christmas had made Charlotte think of the same time last year when they should have been celebrating the promised Allied victory. No-one spoke like that now, except perhaps her mother, who clung to the belief that it would soon be cleared up. It was as if her mother considered the War a nuisance to be got rid of as soon as possible, and it was becoming irksome to her that it seemed it was not being dealt with properly. Her friends in London told her that now the fiery Welshman Lloyd George was the new Prime Minister, and as Sir John French had been replaced as British Commander-in-Chief by Sir Douglas Haig, things would improve. Haig was a distant relative of her cousin, and she felt that he would take a much firmer line. She had said as much to Francis at breakfast this morning. It was her belief that Haig would 'soon sort things out'.

'Haig's idea is to put all manpower to the Western Front,' Francis replied. 'Do you know what that means?'

'Francis, dear, I'm not completely ignorant in these matters,' said his mother. 'He'll concentrate on one area, break through there, and then . . .'

‘And then?’ demanded Francis.

‘They should never have started it in the first place.’ Mrs Armstrong-Barnes’s face was uncompromising. ‘They’ll get what they deserve.’

‘And supposing Haig doesn’t manage to get the Army to “break through”?’ persisted Francis. ‘It has been tried already without success.’

‘He will eventually,’ his mother said patiently. ‘Our men will just keep trying until they do.’

Francis opened his mouth to reply, but at that point Annie came into the room to clear the table. Francis heard Charlotte’s indrawn breath and caught her warning look. Francis looked at Annie and his gaze softened at once.

His mother too was affected by Annie’s presence in the room. ‘No news with the post today?’ she enquired gently.

Annie shook her head. ‘I am not giving up on them, though. I’ve heard that dozens of families from their battalion got the same telegram. We’re hoping that they’ve all managed to stick together somehow, maybe help each other along. Even if they’re badly wounded, as long as they’re with each other they’ll get by.’

Francis stood up, mumbled an excuse, and went quickly out of the room. His eyes were filled with tears.

Mrs Armstrong-Barnes folded her napkin carefully and laid it beside her plate. Then she raised her head and gave her daughter a bright smile.

'Do wrap up well for your walk to the village,' she said.

Charlotte got up, came round the table and kissed her mother. They held hands for a moment. Charlotte had been a little surprised that her mother had raised no objection when she told her of her intention to seek nursing work in the military hospital in the city. She knew that Charlotte did not want to join her round of afternoon teas, and sewing circles. And at first this had been a disappointment to her, for she had imagined that as Charlotte grew older they would shop and socialize together. She had planned to secure her invitations to elegant balls, and that there would be shared card afternoons where Charlotte could be looked over and assessed by prospective mothers-in-law. But many of the young men were on active service, and Charlotte felt that her mother was now secretly proud that her daughter was contributing, especially when Francis was not.

On her bus journey to the city, Charlotte's mind was troubled by thoughts of her brother. To begin with it had been assumed that his commission had been held up, but now she feared that perhaps the village was beginning to gossip about him not being in uniform. His manner worried her. Either he shut himself away with the household accounts or went out early with his sketch-pad, wandered the hills all day and came home with nothing. Francis was still in her thoughts when she got off the bus at the gate of the hospital, and asked the porter the way.

He had to repeat his directions twice, and eventually left the gatehouse and walked across the quadrangle with her to point out the part of the hospital where she was due to report. The porter watched Charlotte's slight figure hurrying across the great open square. 'This damned war has taken our children's innocence,' he muttered as he returned to his post, and picked up his newspaper. 'That one should be at home playing at nursing her dollies. She's too young to see what she's going to see in the wards.'

Chapter 9

LATER THAT DAY, Charlotte, had she been asked, would have agreed with him.

Things went badly for her from the beginning. The hospital was huge and she lost her way. It was fifteen minutes after the appointed time before she found the room where the Staff Sister was briefing the new staff.

As Charlotte tried to slip in unobtrusively the Staff Sister stopped in mid-sentence. She lifted her register. 'You are?'

'Charlotte Armstrong-Barnes. I am sorry I am late.'

'I am the Staff Sister. When you reply to me, you will use my title.' She waited a moment, and as Charlotte said nothing she demanded, 'Miss Armstrong-Barnes, do you understand?'

'Yes,' said Charlotte.

'Obviously not,' said the Staff Sister.

There was a long pause. 'Say "yes, Staff Sister",' hissed a voice in her ear.

'Yes, Staff Sister,' Charlotte stuttered, and gave the girl beside her a grateful look.

'Very good.' The Staff Sister ticked Charlotte's name on a register she held. 'You have nursing qualifications?'

'I have the First Aid, and part of the Home Nursing Certificate,' said Charlotte.

There was a giggle, quickly suppressed, from one of the other nurses.

Charlotte's face felt hot.

'Take your place, and pay attention,' ordered the Staff Sister. 'When we have finished here we will go on a tour of the wards, then you will be assigned duties . . .' Her glance flicked over Charlotte. '. . . appropriate to your qualifications and experience.'

The hospital was obviously very busy. The beds were so close together that staff could scarcely move between them. And as soon as the group of new recruits were familiar with the wards in which they had to work, they had duties assigned.

The Staff Sister scrutinized Charlotte carefully. 'I'd like you to report to Surgical for orderly duties. Sister Bateman will decide what you're fit for.'

In Surgical Sister Bateman looked Charlotte up and down and then at the paper in her hand. 'You are the one from the

Cottage Hospital . . .' She gave a little shake of her head. 'You do appreciate that here we do a bit more than rolling bandages.'

Charlotte blushed but managed to reply in a pleasant voice. 'I think I can cope with whatever you give me to do.'

Sister Bateman raised her eyebrows.

'Sister,' Charlotte added hurriedly.

The Sister's eyes narrowed. 'Let us go to the sluice room attached to the operating theatre,' she said in an equally pleasant voice, 'and we shall see if you can cope with the work there.'

The sluice room was down a flight of stairs and when they arrived there was an older man scrubbing one of the big sinks. He raised his head as Sister Bateman entered.

'Orderly Martin, Miss Armstrong-Barnes has been sent to assist us. Show her how to dispose of the contents of the lidded buckets.' Sister Bateman turned to Charlotte and indicated the bucket she meant. Charlotte went forward and picked up the bucket. Sister Bateman was watching her closely. 'Before disposing of anything, you should always check the contents.' She waited, keeping her eyes on Charlotte's face.

'Sister, if it is her first day, let me—' Orderly Martin began.

The Sister silenced him with a look.

Charlotte lifted the lid of the bucket. It contained a man's arm, severed above the elbow. Charlotte gave out a choking gasp, and dropped the lid back on the bucket.

The Sister nodded her head. 'I thought as much,' she said more to herself than anyone else. 'I'll see that you are transferred to somewhere else,' she said in a louder voice. 'Tea trolley duties would be more suitable for—'

Charlotte had closed her eyes for a moment, but as she heard the Sister speaking she opened them again quickly. She looked up and met the Sister's eyes, interrupting her with a smile. 'This bucket contains an amputated limb,' she said in a steady voice. 'How would you like me to dispose of it?'

The Sister stopped in mid-sentence and waited a moment or two, watching Charlotte carefully. Then she nodded at Orderly Martin and turned and left the room.

Charlotte worked in the sluice room all morning. This must have been what her own matron had meant when she had said that Charlotte would not be protected in the city hospital. If it had not been for the constant cheery presence of Orderly Martin she would probably have run straight back to the Cottage Hospital.

'Don't let Bossy Bateman get you down,' he advised Charlotte. 'She lost her man at Mons, in the very first of the fighting and she's never smiled since, poor love.'

The Surgical Department was busy, and as the operating assistants came and went Charlotte smiled determinedly, and tried not to look at, or think about, what she was handling.

After lunchtime the unit staff were summoned to the Matron's office for a meeting. She had hardly begun when her telephone rang. After listening for a few minutes she replaced the receiver.

'A hospital train has just pulled in at Waverley Station. The wounded men are being brought here. The other city hospitals are full.'

'We're full too,' protested Sister Bateman.

'Well, now we're going to be fuller,' snapped the Matron. 'This is an emergency, the ambulances will be here in minutes. We will use Drill E. You all know what to do.' She looked at Charlotte as everyone else hurried from the room. 'Apart from you, Miss Armstrong-Barnes, and there is no time to instruct you. Let us hope that you prove an asset rather than a liability.'

She assigned Charlotte to basic duties of removing the soiled bandages of the incoming wounded men. 'Unwrap the dressings,' said the Matron, 'and a nurse will come to clean and redress the wound. If you need help, ask. Do not try to cope if you cannot. It only creates more problems.'

The dressing on Charlotte's first patient was days old, and had clearly been applied in a hurry. The blood had congealed to the bandage and as she tried to ease it away a piece of skin came with it. Charlotte felt her insides quiver. She glanced at the man on the bed. His eyes were shut, but she knew by his breathing that he was conscious.

Orderly Martin, who had helped her that morning, was working at the next bed. Charlotte managed to catch his eye.

'*Help*' – she mouthed the word at him.

He came as soon as he could and began to help Charlotte.

As the afternoon passed Charlotte lost all awareness of time. There were so many of them, and they kept coming. Men from all different regiments, Irish Horse, Coldstream Guards, North and South Lancashires. At one point she raised her head and saw that they had begun to place beds down the centre of the ward. If this is happening so far from the Front, what must it be like then in France? she wondered.

'Do you think these are the worst?' she whispered to Orderly Martin as they struggled to cut soiled bandages from one man.

The soldier opened his eyes. 'No, darlin',' he said in a broad Yorkshire accent. 'The worst lie where they fall. Some have been lying where they fell in 1914.'

Charlotte stared at him, not comprehending. What could he possibly mean? He must be delirious. The Army would not leave their dead soldiers just lying around. It was ridiculous. They had their own medical teams: the Royal Army Medical Corps, who attended to the wounded during and after engagements. What the man said could not possibly be true.

Charlotte knew that war must be more bloody than shown in her history books at school where there were paintings of the British Army fighting in the Zulu Wars, Crimea, Waterloo. The orderly ranks were lined up for battle, guns and swords gleaming, horses and men together. It had always looked glorious and exciting. Now that she was grown up, she realized that it couldn't always be like that. She wasn't naïve, she knew that there was blood and gore, and that men died, and horses too. There had been terrible losses in the Crimean War. It was partly reading about Florence Nightingale's work to help the soldiers there that had made her consider doing some nursing. In school they had learned Lord Tennyson's famous poem off by heart. 'Cannon to right of them, cannon to left of them, cannon in front of them volleyed and thundered . . .' It had excited her to think of the spurs jingling, the cries of the men urging their horses on . . . the honour and the glory. But . . . her thoughts faltered, the men of the Light Brigade had been wiped out, and for what? The order to charge should not have been given. It had been a terrible mistake. And yet a poet had turned this dreadful scene into a thing of terrible beauty. She shook her head. Now she was starting to think like Francis. Was all war wrong? Was this war in particular a terrible mistake?

*

By late afternoon Charlotte was exhausted. She was working alone and began to unwrap a dressing when she saw at once there was something seriously wrong. The soldier's leg had been cut off above the knee, but the edges of the wound were moist, swollen and purple. A musty-smelling discharge oozed from between the sutured skin flaps. Charlotte's stomach rose and she thought, I can't cope with this. And then another thought came to Charlotte, clear and distinct. And what is more . . . she thought, *I don't have to.* Her hands paused in mid-air. I will return home, she decided, and that is where I will stay. I can go about with Mother, visiting, and organizing teas. That would be equally helpful, and less distressing for me. She stared at the suppurating wound, and thought, I won't need to see anything like this ever again in my life.

The man on the bed groaned and Charlotte's eyes swivelled from the stinking wound to his face. His skin was ashen, his cheeks and eyes sunken, there was a line down the centre of his forehead where he had set his face against the pain. It was the face of a man aged with suffering, but the patient information card which had arrived with him declared him to be twenty-two years old. She looked around her desperately. The only person she could see was a young doctor, further down the ward. Charlotte signalled for him to come, breathed in and out quickly a few times, and then set to again to remove the old dressing. The soldier grabbed the sleeve of his tunic and bit into it with his teeth.

'This man needs morphine.' The young doctor suddenly appeared by the bed. He put his hand on Charlotte's arm. 'Matron is at the other end of the ward. Fetch her, and have her bring morphine.' He grinned at Charlotte. 'Two Ms. Got it? Matron and morphine. Go.'

For the next half hour or so Charlotte worked with the Matron and the doctor to clean the wound, pack it with sulphonamide powder and set up a drain to take the infection away. When they had finished, the doctor spoke first.

'Sister's office,' he ordered. 'Tea. Now.'

He followed close behind Charlotte and the Matron, and as he entered her office he slammed the door behind him. 'That man is very likely to die! He should not have had a straight-across guillotine amputation. Gangrene tracks back along the muscle. If he had been operated on properly then that wound would have remained clean. What the hell are they doing out there?' he demanded. 'Letting wounded soldiers amputate themselves with their own ruddy bayonets?'

'I've heard they are running out of supplies and are short of staff,' said the Matron as she took the teapot from the little stove in the corner. She waved Charlotte to a seat and handed her a cup of tea.

Charlotte felt her knees begin to tremble and her hand shake so that she could hardly hold her cup.

'You seem calm in a crisis, Armstrong-Barnes,' said the Matron when the doctor had left. 'I think you might be more useful on the wards than in the sluice room. When you are next on duty report directly to me.'

Later when Charlotte went off duty her whole body was trembling with fatigue and nervous strain but there was a glow of triumph within her. She had coped; she had proved herself. She was going to be of use after all.

Chapter 10

A FEW MORNINGS LATER Charlotte went into the library where Francis was sitting reading. He glanced up, acknowledged her presence with a brief grunt and went back to his book. Charlotte wandered over to the window, looked out for a moment or two, and then crossed to the fireplace and began examining objects on the mantelpiece. Francis kept reading.

Charlotte cleared her throat and said, as casually as she could, 'Francis, do you think it at all possible that people from different social stations can get along together?'

Francis didn't lift his head. 'Well, obviously,' he replied. 'We do. In this house, and in the village.'

'What about a deeper, or say, more permanent relationship?'

Francis turned a page. 'Such as?'

Charlotte brushed the skirt of her dress with her hand. 'Ermm . . . marriage for instance.'

Francis barely looked up from his book. 'There is nothing in the law of Church or State to stop them.'

'But does it actually happen?'

'Well, yes. People have in the past, at any rate.'

'I don't mean just technically,' persisted Charlotte. 'I mean, do you think it would work out? Could they be happy?'

Francis closed his book over, finger still in his page. 'There would be huge difficulties . . . money, lifestyle, outlook.' He thought for a long minute. 'But I don't think that is the real issue. It's a huge commitment for two people to agree to be true partners for the rest of their lives, so I think they would both have to have something in common, a shared moral outlook that would bond two people together.'

'Other differences wouldn't matter so much then?'

'Differences can be exciting and stimulating. But when all that first fizzling romance and infatuation burns down, then you need to be able to plant your feet firmly on the bedrock of belief and values.'

'Religious beliefs?'

'No, not necessarily. But I suppose that would help, if it was true belief in the same thing by both parties, and not religion of social convention, or mindless repeated prayer learned by rote. I suppose I really mean common values.'

Francis laughed. 'Though there are lots of other things too, like a shared sense of humour, an ability to get along under duress . . .' He stopped and looked at his sister curiously. 'This is a very serious subject for so early in the morning.'

'Oh,' said Charlotte in an offhand manner, 'it's something that interests me.'

'Why?'

Charlotte turned her face away. 'No reason, in particular,' she said carelessly.

Francis put his book down at once. 'Little sister,' he said teasingly, 'I know you too well. In the space of two minutes, you have asked me half a dozen questions one after the other. There is something on your mind.'

'Oh, it's nothing at all,' said Charlotte quickly. 'The subject was . . . was part of a conversation in the nurses' rest room at the hospital.'

Francis got up from his chair. 'I don't believe you,' he sang out. 'And I'm going to tell Mama, if you don't tell your big brother the truth.'

'It *is* the truth,' Charlotte protested.

Francis came over to the fireplace. 'You always were a hopeless liar, Charlotte. Even when you were little, you could never tell the simplest fib. You were always getting me into the most dreadful trouble. There I would be, making up beautiful stories to cover up for our wrong-doing, and our parents would just turn to you and ask, "Is that correct, Charlotte?" and immediately you would give the game away.'

'Yes, but as I recall, it was mostly *you* who got us into mischief in the first place,' said Charlotte.

'True, true,' said Francis with mock sadness, 'but now you are catching up on lost time.' He folded his arms. 'Tell me, what mischief are you up to today?'

'Nothing,' said Charlotte, as calmly as she could.

Francis peered at her closely. 'Then why is your face pink?' He walked around her. 'That is a *very* pretty dress you have on. Could we be on our way to a secret assignation?' He clapped his hands together. 'I know! John Malcolm Dundas is home on embarkation leave, and you've arranged to see him.'

'Shhh!' Charlotte put her finger to her lips, and glanced anxiously towards the library door which stood ajar.

Francis gasped in pretended horror. 'You mean Mother doesn't know that you are going out unchaperoned to meet a young man!'

'He has so very little time, and has to spend most of it with his family, but he said he would take a walk out to the bridge this morning after breakfast.'

'And you thought that you might just take a stroll down there yourself?' Francis laughed. 'Fortunately it is a bit of a way out of the village, so the gossips won't see you. And Mother hasn't mentioned going out today.'

Charlotte's hand went to her mouth.

Francis laughed. 'Don't worry, little sister. In the unlikely event that Mother decides to go visiting or shopping this morning, I shall ensure that the car won't start until the afternoon.'

Charlotte kissed her brother on his cheek, and darted from the room.

Francis laid the palm of his hand along his cheek where his sister had kissed it, and as he looked after her there was a terrible sadness in his eyes.

Charlotte saw the figure in uniform sitting on the parapet of the bridge, and with a skip of her heart knew that it was John Malcolm. Immediately she slowed down to a demure walk. He must have been looking out for her, for he got to his feet at once, and watched her approach. When she reached him she was still a little out of breath and they stood there, both suddenly shy.

'Hello,' said Charlotte.

John Malcolm only nodded his head, as if the sight of her had made him lose his power of speech.

Charlotte walked all around him as Francis had done with her earlier. 'You look wonderful,' she said sincerely.

John Malcolm nodded again. He was achingly handsome in his uniform, and her breathing felt constricted. 'I brought you something.'

He dragged his eyes from her face to look at her gift. Then he fumbled so awkwardly with the wrapping paper that eventually she took it from him and undid the string herself.

'It's a tea and sugar tin. Look, it has a lid at both ends and is divided in the middle to keep them apart. One side holds tea and the other sugar,' she explained. 'The assistant in the store where I bought it said he had it on authority they were a real boon in the trenches.'

'It's exactly what I need,' he said. He did not tell her that he had already been given two.

'I expect that you've had lots of presents,' said Charlotte.

'Maggie knitted me socks.'

'Oh,' said Charlotte, feeling a little put out that she had been forced by her lack of domestic skills to buy him something rather than make it herself.

'And my father gave me a watch.' John Malcolm took the timepiece from his pocket and showed it to her.

'It's beautiful,' said Charlotte, leaning closer to him.

Their fingers touched, his warm and strong over hers. He grasped her hand in one of his and with the other slipped the watch back into his pocket.

'Charlotte,' he said. 'It might be months, years even, before we see each other again.'

She said nothing, but her eyes began to fill with tears. Impulsively she flung her arms around his chest and felt the rough khaki against her cheek. He responded by holding her there imprisoned in his arms. Charlotte raised her head to look up at him. His eyes were the colour of dark green glass. Her own opened wider as she gazed into his. Then he bent his head and kissed her.

Charlotte thought she would die.

He broke away first, his face flushed.

'I'm sorry,' he said.

'I'm not.' She laid her head back on his chest.

He smiled and she felt the tension ebb out of his body.

'I do like you an awful lot.'

'I know,' she whispered.

'I was hoping that when I come back . . .' He stopped. He looked at her, searching her face. His face was red again. 'I was hoping—'

She put her finger to his lips. 'There will be time enough to talk about it when you come back,' she said.

'Will you write to me?' he asked her.

'You will need to write to me first, so that I will have the address.'

'Don't expect much,' he said. 'I wasn't very good at school learning. Maggie and Alex are the clever ones in our house.'

'It doesn't matter,' said Charlotte. 'Write anyway. I want to know everything you are doing. I want to imagine I'm there with you.'

He gripped her hand tightly and they sat on the wall of the bridge, fingers interlaced, both believing it to be the happiest day of their life.

Chapter 11

JOHN MALCOLM'S LETTERS home to his family were brief, and with a very practical outlook. Despite the fact that she now worked in the munitions factory and had first-hand knowledge of armaments, Maggie couldn't help but note that her twin brother addressed anything of import to her father or Alex. She and her mother received news about the weather or requests for items to be sent on. Her father and Alex discussed battle tactics and how the world would be after the end of the War.

'There's never been a war like this,' Maggie's father declared, 'and there never will be again.'

This made Alex all the more determined to be ready to join up and he wished each night before he went to sleep that it would not be over before he was old enough to do this. He wrote to his older brother begging for every detail of his life in the Army. John Malcolm replied by copying out sections of his Recruit Training in special letters for Alex. Alex seized on the letters as soon as they arrived and read them out importantly.

'*A recruit must develop a soldierly manner and spirit. There must be smartness in turnout and in obeying orders. Personal cleanliness is to be maintained at all times, especially care of the feet.*'

'Well good,' commented Maggie. 'There will be no problems now in getting you to have a bath once a week.'

Alex made a face at her and continued reading. '*A recruit must learn marching, march disciplines, and running. A recruit must be able to take his place in the ranks of his company in close and extended order drill.*'

Alex was thrilled when John Malcolm eventually wrote to say that he and Eddie Kane had been passed as trained men. His father gave him sheets of brown paper from the shop and Alex drew dozens of sketches of soldiers and their equipment. He had made a series of diagrams showing the correct positions for saluting and presenting arms and practised these earnestly each day.

Maggie also noticed that her father had moved automatically for conversation about the War and politics to her younger brother. It was not that he did not discuss events with her or her mother, it was just that the manner of his doing so was more of a lecture, with them being allowed to raise points or ask questions. This began to annoy her. Another source of irritation occurred on the occasions she still helped out in the shop. Charlotte often came in, and in her bright happy fashion chatted about the letters she received from John Malcolm. She would buy lots of little things to send to him, accompanying her purchases with remarks like, 'I am going to send him some fine soap. John Malcolm mentioned that the army soap does not lather well,' or, 'I thought it would be nice to send him some chocolate. He says the food is very plain.'

There was such joy in Charlotte when she spoke about John Malcolm, and her obvious delight at being able to help him in any way made Maggie feel churlish about her resentment of the younger girl. Maggie found that her annoyance was not long lasting, but it was there none the less and she masked it with a cold politeness. When Francis was with Charlotte it was more difficult for Maggie to maintain her coolness. She usually left her father or Alex to attend Charlotte, while she spoke to Francis.

Her continued reading of the newspaper each evening resulted in her having the ability to hold a meaningful discussion with him on current affairs. Francis did not seem surprised by her knowledge, as her father had been when she mentioned that she knew of the use of poison gas, but instead he went into serious detail. Maggie found that she was reading more and in greater depth in order to keep up with him, using her break time in the factory to look at newspapers her father would not stock. As the War progressed he had added to the range of papers sold in the shop, but it was titles such as the *War Illustrated* which were almost jingoistic in their sentiments. He did not take any political journals which had views that he frowned upon. When Maggie thought about some of the radical ideas put forward in their pages she found that they struck a chord within her, and Francis seemed to have a wide knowledge of them all. Unlike her father, he was eager to talk to her about the concept of socialism and pacifist ideals, and also, unlike her father, he did not mind her disagreeing with him. She enjoyed their animated discussions and the fact that neither of them felt threatened by the other when they held opposing opinions. On one occasion she felt quite exhilarated when he had slightly altered his stance in the face of her argument.

One evening on return from her work in the factory she met him on the point of leaving the shop. Francis had stopped at the entrance to wait for his sister, unfolding the evening newspaper as he did so. An item must have caught his eye because she saw him look at the front page and utter an exclamation.

'What is it?' Maggie asked, stopping in the doorway.

'Nothing much,' Francis replied briefly.

Finding the tone of his voice a little strange, Maggie looked at him more closely. She saw that Charlotte too had turned from the counter where Alex was wrapping her purchases.

'It's just another military law,' Francis added lightly.

Charlotte tilted her head to one side. 'What?' she asked her brother. 'A military law about what?'

'Conscription,' said Francis.

Chapter 12

THE MILITARY SERVICE Act was enforced on 9 February 1916, compelling single men and childless widowers between the ages of eighteen and forty-one to enlist. Not long after, Francis received his call-up papers. He lodged an appeal and was called to a Military Tribunal in Edinburgh.

When Francis arrived at Military Headquarters he was met by an officer who introduced himself as Major Grant, a cousin of his father. 'Unfortunately I am not sitting on today's tribunal, but your mother asked me to have a word with you before you were called in. I have it to understand that you are looking for an exemption.'

Francis replied. 'I suppose that I must be,' he said. 'At any rate I do not want to enlist.'

'It may be that there are grounds that would suffice. You are engaged in some vital industrial skill?'

Francis looked at his hands. 'Hardly.'

The Major frowned. 'You do appreciate that volunteers can choose which regiment to be attached to? If you are conscripted then you must go where you are sent.' He paused. 'It would be better if you chose to enlist.'

'I cannot do that,' said Francis. 'If I am compelled to take up arms then perhaps I must. But I will not choose of my own free will to fight in this war.'

'It can be very difficult for a man whom they think is a Conchie, or . . . worse.'

Francis spoke in a low voice. 'I know. I have heard that conscientious objectors are sent as stretcher-bearers into No Man's Land in the thick of the fighting.'

'That could be the least of it. If they deem you to be a malingerer you could be sent to prison or to a labour camp. Men have died or gone mad in these camps. Can you say that you are a pacifist? Are you of a Quaker persuasion?'

'I cannot say that,' said Francis. 'I am not a conscientious objector. I agree that it may be necessary to kill if the cause is just.'

'Killing is required in war.'

'This cause is not just,' said Francis passionately. 'The War should be stopped at once. The vast amounts of money maintaining the Army would be better spent at home feeding the poor. It is the same situation in Germany, and the condition of the ordinary Russian people does not bear thinking about. Thousands of young men's lives are being squandered for little gain.'

'The conduct of the War is criticized in many places,' replied the Major. 'Mostly by those who know nothing of warfare. It is true that mistakes have been made, but we have learned from them.'

'Other men pay with their lives for your mistakes,' Francis said bitterly. 'The carnage sickens me.'

'Things are improving,' said Major Grant.

'How can a war *improve*?' said Francis in despair.

'If you are not a Conchie, what are you, man?' demanded the Major.

After some moments' thought, Francis said, 'I am a human being who does not believe in killing my fellow man for insufficient reason.'

The Major made an impatient gesture. 'You may not realize it, but the objections you give would, in some quarters, be thought of as talking treason.'

'I must answer as truthfully as I can.'

The Major sighed. 'How young you are. It does not always do to be . . . completely truthful.'

'It is the way I am,' said Francis.

As he left the room Major Grant put his hand on Francis's shoulder. 'For your mother's sake, I beg you to say as little as possible.'

The tribunal gave Francis four minutes of their time before declaring him suitable to be called up. Then much to Francis's embarrassment a letter from Major Grant was read aloud. In it he stated that, as a friend of the family, he felt it his duty to inform the tribunal that the management of Stratharden was beyond the capability of Mrs Armstrong-Barnes. Her son was needed to oversee the workings of the estate and a good part of the economy of the village depended on the estate. The tribunal then agreed, on both domestic and business grounds, to grant Francis a temporary exemption.

Francis came out into Wellington Square feeling helpless and disorientated. He began to walk aimlessly through the city. A number of his friends and relatives lived in Edinburgh, and in the past he would have visited them or even stayed the night. But by now most had enlisted, some had already been killed, and he was aware that if he called upon their families it might prove awkward and uncomfortable. By late afternoon he found himself on the outskirts of the city, and knowing that the country bus must stop at some point along this route on its way to Stratharden, he decided to return home. He noticed a group of workers and shoppers waiting on the pavement opposite, and saw that one of them was Margaret Dundas. He crossed the road and asked if he might stand with her.

'Are you not travelling by car today?' Maggie asked Francis, more for something to say than anything else.

Francis shook his head. 'I deemed it an unwise thing to do.'

Maggie nodded her agreement. 'Yes, saving on fuel is sensible when the troops at the Front are so short of supplies.'

Francis gave her a quirky look. 'It was more to do with the fact that I was at Military Headquarters in Edinburgh today attending a tribunal that wanted to discuss my refusal to enlist for military service.'

'Oh,' said Maggie.

'"Oh," indeed,' said Francis. 'Some of the chaps there have been at the Front, suffering God knows what kind of deprivation. I thought it would be tremendously bad form to roll up in a large motor car. It might have given them the wrong impression altogether.'

Maggie couldn't help but laugh out loud.

Francis put his head on one side and looked at her. 'Laughing suits you,' he said.

Maggie looked at him quickly, suspecting that he was mocking her. The grey eyes looking back at her seemed sincere. She could feel herself beginning to blush. 'Tell me about the tribunal,' she asked quickly.

Francis told her of his conversation with his father's cousin, who had warned him against saying too much.

'The tribunal itself was a formality,' he went on. 'The Colonel in charge as good as said so. He said that they were desperately short of men in France and that it did not serve the national interest to give complete exemptions.'

'What did you say?' Maggie asked him.

'Only that I did not think it was a just cause. To which they concluded that the war would be lost if everyone cared as little as I did.' Francis turned a desperate face to Maggie. 'It's not because I don't care,' he said in a wretched voice. 'Rather, it's because I *do*.'

Maggie looked at him, and was aware of some great distress within him. 'I don't doubt it,' she said.

There was a silence where Francis saw that this girl was the first and only person who had freely accepted his standpoint. 'Thank you,' he said at last, and then after a moment, 'but it must be difficult for you to appreciate this point of view when your brother volunteered and is now fighting in France.'

'My brother's viewpoint is not necessarily mine,' said Maggie. 'And to hold one viewpoint does not mean that one cannot be in sympathy with another's.'

Francis smiled and gave a slight inclination of his head. Then his eyes narrowed as he looked beyond Maggie towards the others waiting for the bus.

Maggie turned her head. Two women, both dressed in black, were walking slowly along the pavement, stopping to speak to each group or individual. As they came nearer Francis took a step away from Maggie to put a little distance between himself and her. The women stopped in front of him and the older of the two addressed Francis. 'Not wearing khaki, sir?'

'How observant you are,' Francis replied quietly.

'Officers on leave tend to wear their uniform.'

'I am neither an officer, nor am I on leave,' Francis replied.

The woman turned to her younger companion. 'I thought as much,' she said. She nodded her head.

The younger woman took a white feather from the little straw basket she carried and held it in front of Francis's face. He lowered his eyes, and the onlookers began to nudge each other and whisper together. Maggie's cheeks flamed red, and she moved quickly to Francis's side as the two women began to talk to each other in a loud tone of voice.

'It is usually very easy to tell the type of man who will not join up,' said the older woman. 'They have a certain weakness in their features.'

'Cowards cannot hide their cowardice!' the young woman cried out in a shrill voice.

'They pretend it is a matter of conscience to be excused,' said the older one.

'Nothing can excuse them. Others perish while they sit happily at home.' The younger woman's eyes were now full of tears and her face had taken on a blotched appearance.

Francis gravely took the white feather from her.

'Wear that badge of shame, so that all might know you for what you are!' The younger woman almost spat at Francis.

The older woman took the younger woman's arm and led her away.

'How dare they!' cried Maggie. 'You could be in a reserved occupation, or ill, or wounded.'

'How noble you are, Maggie,' said Francis. 'Most of my other friends would not defend me. And,' he waved his hand towards the people around, 'everyone else here is cringing away.'

'Well I'm not.' Maggie tucked her arm into his. 'Your reasons for not fighting make a lot of sense to me. The behaviour of those two women is outrageous.'

'No doubt they have their reasons,' said Francis. 'The younger one looked close to breaking down. I would say that she has recently lost a new husband, and her companion is the boy's mother.'

Maggie fell silent for a moment. 'You are so generous in your understanding,' she said at last. 'I would condemn them as easily as they condemn you.'

'I am becoming accustomed to it when I am out in public. I have quite a collection of white feathers now.'

He smiled down at her. Maggie was suddenly aware that he had a firm hold of her elbow, but that it was she who had boldly taken his arm in the first place. They weren't so close by kin or by attachment to make this conduct correct, especially in public. It felt vaguely improper, but she wasn't quite sure how to disentangle herself, and indeed whether it would now be rude to do so. At that moment the bus arrived, and by her feeling of swift disappointment Maggie realized that she did not particularly want to relinquish her hold of Francis's arm.

Later that night, when she recalled their conversation, Maggie knew that her response at the bus stop had been genuine. She did not in any way consider Francis a coward. It seemed to her a brave thing for him to do, to refuse to enlist knowing that he would be called upon to explain it, be misjudged by others, and even jeered at by strangers. She felt confused. Her brother had gone off to fight for King and Country. She was proud of him, and agreed with her father when he said that Britain had a duty to use her might and strength to help her Allies. Small countries like Belgium needed protection from greedy powers who would take away their land and freedom. And yet, Francis might be right when he said that it was a colossal waste of money and lives.

It must be tremendously difficult for him. Word would leak out and the villagers would begin to talk. It had always been accepted that he was waiting for his commission, but now he would become the target of gossip. They would say that his position had made it easier for him to get an exemption. This was true, and yet that had not been of his choosing. Indeed, the method of obtaining the exemption had effectively disempowered him of his own protest. Obviously his mother was concerned about his position as a non-combatant, and had discussed with a relative, Major Grant, the best way to deal with it. Maggie doubted if Francis discussed his feelings even with Charlotte. He knew of his sister's attachment to John Malcolm, and was sensitive enough to see that it would be inappropriate of him to condemn the War as John Malcolm was now on his way to the Front. By his remark today she was sure that Francis had found little sympathy elsewhere. He had mentioned his other friends not defending him. And as this thought entered her head Maggie realized with slight surprise that Francis looked upon her as a friend.

Chapter 13

CHARLOTTE SNATCHED up the letter from the hall table. She began to open it and then stopped. Her mother was about the house somewhere, and Charlotte knew that she would think that she was perfectly entitled to read any mail that her daughter received. She might in fact deem it more proper that she read it first. Charlotte decided to walk down to the bridge. It was there that John Malcolm had met her and Francis when he had run so hard to catch up with her on the day of their first walk alone together. It was there that they had said goodbye to each other. She would go there where she could be private. Charlotte tucked the letter in the pocket of her dress, slipped quietly from the house, and hurried down the drive. When she reached the bridge she settled herself on the parapet and tore the envelope open. John Malcolm's last letter had said that he was soon to be sent out in a draft to join the regiment's 1st Battalion, so this must have been written from somewhere across the Channel.

Dear Charlie,

he began. Charlotte hugged the letter to her. She loved his special name for her. No-one, not even Francis, had ever called her that. It was special from him to her.

Here we are at last, and theres lots to tell you since my last letter, but the main thing is that me and Eddie are having the most tremendous time. Crossing the Channel was rough (although the real soldiers on the boat only lafed when they saw our faces turning green!) I have only a faint memory of the famus cliffs of Dover, more grey than white as I recal. Yours truly didn't see much of them as he was heaving up in a bucket. What didnt help a lot was that we all had a huge breakfast before leaving. The barracks did us proud on our last morning and every man had as much fried eggs and bread and dripping as they could manage. Most were sick over the side, or as near as they could get. Our Company Sergeant had no pity and sent us to clean it up and said that if we knew we had to mop up our breakfast then it might make us hold it down in future! And then someone shouted they could see land, and we all rushed to the rails and there it was – France!

Charlotte raised her head from reading for a moment. John Malcolm was in France! He was actually there! She knew that he would be so thrilled to be going to the Front with his battalion that part of her shared his excitement.

And very green and pleasant it looked. And all along the cliffs for miles and miles, were the troop tents and the white tops of hospital margees.

There were some days spent in training in Etaples, and then we got word it was our turn to go down to where our trenches are. We gave a mighty roar when we heard this because we've been raring to go and the training and the drilling is grim, and goes on and on. Next thing was we were crammed onto the train for Doullens to take us nearer to where the action is. It was glorius weather when we got there too glorius in fact for we now had to march quite a long way to the village where our billet is. The French roads are cobbled close set with large shiny stones and is the very devil to walk on as it is so uneven we slip and slide in our great hob-nailed boots draged down with heavy packs. As well as our personal stuff, we've got arms and ammunition and rations – corned beef and hard biscuits – and a mess tin for warming our food (do let Maggie know that when I'm at the front I might have to do some cooking!) We've also to carry a shovel wire cutters and other things a gas mask and then on top of all that is our steel helmet. These last two items we've been told NOT to lose, as our lives might depend on them one day. Our Sergeant keeps a sharp eye as it seems that to save carying so much, men have been known to drop off items by the side of the road, and he's asured us it's fearful trouble if we do.

We marched along cheerily enough folowing behind the Major in charge of our Battalion he led the way on his fine horse setting us a fairly brisk pace it was very hot and dusty all morning, and hotter and dustier as the day went on. We are a sturdy bunch of chaps and kept up with (almost!) no moaning, but as time went on I have to say we were begining to straggle out a bit.

And now I must tell you what happened as evening came on. We were getting near the village when we saw in the distance a large group of men approaching. They turned out to be men of the West Yorkshire Regiment who had been in the thick of it a few days before. What a bedraggled bunch they looked as they came towards us! stumbling, heads down, many walking wounded supporting each other – thick clay caked over their boots and puttees, their faces dirty. We felt mighty proud tramping smartly on the road, badges and boots shining in late sunshine. Our Major drew up his horse, called the Regimental Sergeant Major forward and spoke to him. The Sergeant Major ran back to us and began yelling . . . "You miserable-green-behind-the-ears-bunch-of-little-boys! There are fighting troops approaching! These men have kept the Hun at bay while you played football and cricket at home! You will fall in and present arms! You will salute this battalion of soldiers as if it was the king himself!"

And he had us fall in, and prepare to present arms to them as they came by. We had moved to each side of the road to give them the main highway, and were lined along it like a guard of honour. On they came up the road still faltering, and at last caught sight of us. Then the West Yorkshire's to a man straitened up, dragging themselves into better formation, lifting their heads, raising their weary arms to return the salute. And suddenly from our men's throats a great cheer went up, loud and long. It must have lifted their hearts I know it did mine. And the Yorkshire men began to call to us, winking and shouting . . . "Give 'em hell when you get there, boys" and "Don't let them gain an inch," and one man pointed to his filthy boots and cried out, "It may be mud and dirt, but it's <u>our</u> mud and dirt, and they're not having it!" Everybody laughed then, and the Yorkshire men began to sing, "Pack up your troubles in your old kit bag, and smile, boys, smile. While you've a lucifer to light *your fag, smile boys, that's the style . . ." and our lot joined in, and the last of them went past and still we could hear the tramp of their boots, and then they struck up, "It's a long way to Tipperary, it's a long way to go . . ."*

We reformed and the Sergeant, who doesn't often praise us said, "Well done lads. Well done", and the Major nodded once or twice, and he turned his horse's head, and we went off down that road in the setting sun singing our hearts out.

He finished by telling her not to worry about him, and that he thought about her every day.

Charlotte adored John Malcolm's letters to her. There was nothing at all shocking in them, but there was an almost illicit thrill in her receiving letters from a soldier at the Front, his occasional misspelled words making them even more endearing to her. She had begun to reread parts of the letter when she heard footsteps on the bridge, and looked up. It was Margaret Dundas. Charlotte was so happy, she felt that everyone else should be happy too. She gave John Malcolm's sister a bright smile.

Maggie nodded in reply. 'A pleasant evening,' she said. She did not add the word 'miss' at the end, as her father or mother would have done, thinking, I refuse to greet this girl in this way, just because she has wealth and position.

Charlotte jumped down. 'Yes, it is,' she agreed happily. 'It is a very pleasant evening.' She waved her letter at Maggie. 'John Malcolm writes that he is in France! Isn't it exciting!'

Maggie saw the letter in Charlotte's hand. It seemed bulkier than those they received at home. Her brother was writing longer letters to Charlotte than to his own family! A little twist of jealousy entered Maggie's mood. It would seem that John Malcolm had more to say to Charlotte than to his own sister. 'Yes, we know that,' she said brusquely. 'He has written to tell us.'

Charlotte appeared not to notice anything offputting in Maggie's manner. 'Are you going to the farm?' she asked, and as Maggie nodded, she went on, 'May I walk with you part of the way?'

Maggie smiled a tight smile and said yes. I can't very well say 'no, go away', she thought to herself, which is what she would have liked to have done.

By the time Charlotte had said goodbye at the end of the avenue to the big house Maggie was in a thorough ill humour. She had begun her own walk in a mood of resentment and Charlotte chattering on about John Malcolm's letter only made her worse. It was really Alex's fault that she was so out of sorts, she decided as she returned home. When she next saw him she would clip his ear. She had been required to walk out the mile or so to the farm with the milk order because he had run off somewhere with his pals to play football.

But Alex was not playing football. He was engaged in more serious business altogether. As April moved into May, and then June followed, the evenings drew out and the boys were allowed to play outside later each night. Alex, with his friend Hugh Kane and a few other boys from the village, had decided to undertake a programme of military training. With luck the War would go on a bit longer and then they could go off and join their brothers. Meanwhile they would train themselves up so that they would be ready.

Alex and Hugh were the leaders and nobody dared to challenge them. Alex had paper and pencils from his father's shop to write down his orders, and he was able to filch supplies which served as army rations. Hugh had a helmet from the Boer War where his father had fought and died. Both boys had letters from their brothers describing the training given at the army camps in England and in France, which they were using to instruct their own recruits.

Upstream from the village they had made an army dug-out with old pieces of wood under the large rhododendron bushes which bordered the Strathardin estate. Here they drilled and marched under Alex and Hugh's critical observation and now knew most of the commands. They stood to attention, presented arms, and enacted the morning and evening 'stand to arms' as their brothers had told them was done in the trenches every morning and evening. An old potato sack stuffed with straw hung from a tree and they practised bayonet charges with long wooden sticks. Tea was brewed up over small fires with water gathered from the river in tin mugs.

After the other boys went home Alex sat down with his back against one of the trees. His face, which was longer and thinner than John Malcolm's, wore a grave expression. He pulled out a notebook and a pencil stub to mark up his own progress. Ten counts to run around the field. This was an improvement on his last time. Five counts to climb the oak tree. This was the same, but he had not felt so sick when looking down at the ground, so that could be marked up as an improvement. He awarded himself another tick. He looked at his body critically. Stripped to the waist most afternoons, his chest and arms were turning brown under the summer sun. He was sure that he looked more mature than he did a few months ago, but knew that his build was still more of a boy than a man.

His boxing lessons with Hugh were not going well at all. Despite Alex being tall for his age, Hugh was a half a head taller still and his reach was longer. Although Alex could hit harder he seldom could get near enough to land the punch. He needed a strategy to help overcome this. Alex thought carefully and then wrote out in his book 'eat more'. He underlined it twice. It might be difficult as more and more food was being rationed, and there were shortages. He'd heard that the Army no longer turned down men who didn't pass the medical examination; still, he was determined to be fit enough to enlist as soon as he was old enough. His one great hope was to be put in the same battalion as his brother. You could ask to be put in the same regiment as friends or relations, loads of boys had done that already. Alex marked the date in his notebook, 9 June 1916. He would soon be fifteen. He frowned as he tucked the book and pencil into his trouser pocket. Three years was an age to wait to go to France and fight side by side with his brother. At the moment even his sister, who was a girl, was doing more than him.

Chapter 14

WORKING IN THE Springbank Munitions Factory tired Maggie out. The summer weather was becoming hot and the atmosphere among the machines was stifling. Eight-hour shifts of heavy work left her bones aching, and her muscles groaning for a hot bath and a liniment rub. She had been used to long hours in the shop, but it had always been her dad and John Malcolm who had done the heavy work. They dealt with the delivery and despatch of provisions, loading and unloading the carts and barrows. Maggie now realized what they had been sparing her. She paused for a moment, arched her shoulders and stretched her back.

Clara, who worked the machine beside her, laughed and nodded towards the factory clock. 'Not long to go,' she shouted above the noise of the machines.

Although grubby and sore, Maggie smiled back. Even after weeks at the munitions factory her arms and shoulders still ached at the end of each day, and, despite the protective cap and clothes she wore, her face and hair were filmed with fine dust. Yet she was more content than she had been working in her father's shop, although when she took time to think about this she was unsure why.

There was the gratifying knowledge that you were contributing directly to the war effort. A tally of their output was displayed on boards, and there was fierce competition among the machine shops to better each other's totals. But factory work was monotonous, noisy and dirty, far removed from the genteel respectability of the shop. Being among hundreds of people and hearing the familiar way the men and women joked with each other had been a difficult adjustment for Maggie to make. Even now she did not feel completely part of this collection of chattering girls, older women, men and young lads, with varieties of ways of dress, speech and manners. Coming from a rural village where things moved more slowly and old customs were kept, to a more modern environment which itself was changing swiftly, was strange and confusing.

At first Maggie was slightly shocked by the sights she had seen when travelling through the town. In the main railway station where many women stood saying goodbye to their menfolk, she had seen a couple who were obviously unmarried kissing each other on the mouth! – in public! – apparently unconcerned about the stares they were attracting. In the city also, women's clothes were different. There were still plenty of older working-class women wrapped in plaids, 'shawlies', her mother would have called them. But each day more and more ladies, in all walks of life, were wearing dresses swept up at the hemline, with wider fuller skirts, which revealed their ankles and stockings. Young women were beginning to move about more freely on the streets. Quite elegant women were seen chatting and shopping, unescorted by a man or an older woman.

Not long after Maggie had started working, as she and Clara had waited together one afternoon at the bus stop, there had been a woman ahead of them in the queue, smoking. Clara saw Maggie staring. She nudged her. 'Takes a bit of getting used to,' she said.

'There is a lot to get used to,' replied Maggie. 'I feel like such a country cousin.'

'It's not so much to do with being from the country,' said Clara. 'Things are changing so fast, you can hardly keep up. My mother is not happy about me mixing with the opposite sex without her there. She thinks that talking to a man is equal to becoming engaged.'

'I saw a woman and a man kissing each other,' said Maggie, 'right in front of everyone. I suppose,' she added slowly, 'that it *was* in the railway station . . . and he was a soldier going off to war.'

'If I got half a chance *I'd* kiss a soldier,' said Clara, 'whether he was going off to war or not.' And she giggled with laughter.

Maggie smiled in spite of herself. This was a subject that both her mother and father had lectured her on when they realized her mind was made up and she was going to work in the city. She had to beware of 'loose morals' among certain types of people. Her mother had given her grave warnings about 'losing her character'. As far as Maggie could see, the morals of one type of person were pretty much like those of any other. Although perhaps those with more money were more adept at concealing their misdemeanours. 'My mother constantly nags me about keeping bad company,' said Maggie.

'I don't tell my mother all that goes on during or outside working hours,' said Clara.

And Maggie soon found that she was doing the same. At home there were things she didn't mention. The gossip in the girls' cloakrooms or the after-hours socializing, when little groups of girls would go with some of the young lads into the nearby public houses. Her parents would sometimes comment on how tired she looked; her mother in particular often asked her when she intended to give it up, and come back to the shop where she belonged: Maggie tried to avoid answering questions like this because they invariably led to arguments.

'I don't *belong* in the shop,' she once told her mother sharply.

Her mother was astounded. 'Of course you do, dear. Your father owns the shop,' she added, as though that fact logically explained her first remark.

'I should be able to choose what I want to do,' Maggie said.

'Only the very rich can choose what they want to do,' her mother replied. 'The rest of us occupy our set station in life, and you should be grateful to have one which feeds and clothes you.'

Maggie ground her teeth and said nothing more, but when she told Clara of this conversation her friend became quite serious.

'That's one thing this war has done which is for the good. There can be no more talk of keeping to your place. I won't live my life at someone else's beck and call.'

It was a subject that Maggie often heard discussed in the factory. Without the munitions industry most of the working girls would have become maids or something similar. The factory had attracted people from all walks of life, many former domestic servants who had left a life of drudgery.

'Never again will I run when I hear a bell,' one of the older women said.

Maggie thought of Stratharden House, known to the villagers as the 'Big House'. Maggie knew several of the people employed there as servants, but apart from small grumbles she had not heard many complaints about their working conditions. Mrs Armstrong-Barnes was considered remote but gracious, Charlotte unassuming, and Francis had always just been . . . Francis. Maggie had never really thought out before the consequences of having a domineering or unkind employer. It must be truly awful to be so financially dependent on someone as to have to tolerate personal disrespect. Her position in the shop was not that of an equal but she knew that her father, even though he expected it as a duty, did value her contribution. But the work she did now was completely different. The employers demanded hard work, but the workers were paid for it in cash, not in bondage conditions where you could be tied for food, and accommodation.

'After the War is over, they won't need us here,' one of the girls said. 'And then we'll have to go back and do what we did before. At the moment they're desperate, but wait until the War ends.'

'It doesn't need to be like that,' said Clara. 'Every day the newspapers carry columns of advertisements for all kinds of help. Workers are needed to keep the country going, so if they join together then they would have power. We can't have proper representation here because they've put the factory under military law. But after the War I'm going to join a trade union. That way you have someone to speak up for you about wages and conditions.'

Maggie had only vaguely thought about this. The fact that there was a war to be fought and won made it seem slightly disloyal to be thinking about yourself.

Clara laughed at this. 'That's the way they want you to think. Then you'll keep on working without complaining. This place is not too bad but there are other factories where the equipment is unsafe and there have been explosions, and some of the chemicals cause poisoning.'

Maggie realized that these topics were similar to those that Francis Armstrong-Barnes talked about. She had always thought of his conversations as some kind of elevated theoretical discussion, not in any way practically applicable. Now that she could see where it might involve an actual struggle for power, she had a disturbing fleeting moment of fear. These were the politics of dissension. This was dangerous. Strikers on Clydeside had been arrested for obstructing the production of armaments. It was yet another subject that she could not comfortably discuss at home. On her bus journeys she often read the pamphlets Clara gave her, but tucked them deep down in her bag before reaching the village.

She was reading one in early summer on her way home when the bus halted outside Springbank Hospital and Charlotte got on.

'May I sit with you?' she asked Maggie.

Maggie moved to make room on the seat.

As if to explain herself Charlotte said, 'I worked later today. The wards are so busy. There seems to be no end to the wounded.'

The younger girl's face was pale. She looks as tired as I feel, thought Maggie, and she could not help asking Charlotte why she had left the easier life of the Cottage Hospital.

Charlotte shrugged. 'The same reason that you are in munitions work, I suppose. One is trying to help as best one can.'

Maggie was curious. 'Didn't your mother object to you going to work in the city?'

'Not so much as she might have . . .' Charlotte hesitated and looked at Maggie. She *was* John Malcolm's sister. She should be able to speak freely about Francis to her, and the village probably talked about him anyway. 'Because of my brother Francis, you understand. His not being in any of the armed forces makes my mother . . . uncomfortable. Everyone else is doing so much, I think my mother is glad that I am contributing.'

'Your brother has convictions which prevent him from fighting,' Maggie said at once.

Charlotte blinked at her intensity, and Maggie realized how quickly she had rushed to defend Francis.

'He has had discussions with me . . .' Maggie went on awkwardly, '. . . and with my father, in the shop, talking about the rights and wrongs of the War.'

'Yet your brother, John Malcolm, believes in it absolutely.'

Once again Maggie felt irritation at Charlotte's familiarity with her brother.

'He is quite taken up with it all,' Charlotte continued, 'and I must confess, his letters do make it sound very exciting. But many of our soldiers are being killed or wounded.'

'Yes,' said Maggie, thinking to herself that perhaps she had misjudged this girl. Charlotte's joyous youth masked a more thoughtful person. 'Your hospital work must let you see that we are not always victorious.'

There was silence between them for a while, and then Charlotte spoke. 'I have heard you speak with my brother, and I know that you read a lot and keep up with what is happening.'

She turned to Maggie. 'Do you think that what we hear is true? That there will be one great battle this summer and then it will be finished?'

'I don't know,' said Maggie. 'There are those who are very confident, and there are those who say it cannot happen all at once, because Germany has prepared so well for any attack.'

'It's just that . . .' Charlotte continued slowly. 'I am very proud that John Malcolm is in the Army, and glad that he is doing what he wants to do, but . . . now I wish it was all over and that he was home again.'

Maggie heard the unspoken fear in what Charlotte had just said. She too was concerned for her brother's safety. She smiled, and said, as much to reassure herself as Charlotte, 'Perhaps what you hear is true. It may be that this coming battle will be the one that ends the War.'

Chapter 15

THERE WAS NO doubt in the mind of the Commanding Officer of John Malcolm's company, newly promoted Captain Tim Bradley. This next engagement would be the one in which he would lead his men to glory. A volunteer like most of his men, he was a replacement for an officer killed at Gallipoli, and was thrilled that he had reached the Front in time to take part in the coming battle. After a short introductory spell in a quiet sector of the forward lines, the 1st Battalion was now back behind the lines and engaged in training or helping with preparations for the big push.

Where they were stationed, north of the river Somme, was crowded with men and equipment, the roads thronged with lorries, gun limbers, food supply wagons and ammunition carts. Every possible army service was being set up over a wide area: mining, signalling, air reconnaissance, accompanied by scores of administration units. Chinese and Indian workers hurried about and the soldiers marched on fatigues, digging gun pits, laying lines for narrow-gauge railways to transport enormous masses of food and fuel to the Front.

There was a huge training ground, part of which had been set up to resemble No Man's Land and the German trenches, where officers and men were briefed on their objectives. As they waited behind the lines John Malcolm Dundas and Eddie Kane trained with the rest of their company and watched soldiers and workers from every part of the British Empire. The air throbbed with the sound of the guns. In the last days of a hot June an unceasing bombardment pounded the enemy. By night the earth glowed and flashed with the crack of exploding shells, by day the sky shook like hammered tin.

In a mood of expectancy and happiness John Malcolm wrote home:

Dear Charlie,

We're here – not allowed to say where – but I've met lots of lads from other regiments. I wish so much I'd got here earlier. They have such great times together and have organized football competitions. It is such a magnifisent thing to have so many friends and companions and know that you are here to fight for your country. Behind the lines there is such a carry on. Some rations are in short supply and we scavenge from other billets, each man trying to find titbits. One of the men came back the other day with chocolate and tins of condensed milk – not enough for everyone to have a share so we thought the best thing to do was to play a game for them. We had to deside what. Cards were out, as some of these boys are sharp and everyone complains of the marked deck. Then any skilled sport – goal scoring or cricket or any such other – was not allowed because one might be better at sport than another. So, you'll never believe this, in the end we played marbles. Everyone stared – the sight of us grown men in uniform crouched down shouting and yelling and getting red in the face over a game of marbles. The Captain came by, and had to have all the noise explained to him, and off he went shaking his head, but the next thing we heard was that by sundown marbles were being played in the officers mess! I didn't win anything I'm sorry to say, but no-one who lost out minded much as we all had such fun.

The guns sound off most of the time, ours and theirs. There is a frightful clatter. You have to learn not to jump as the seasoned troops laf at us Kitchener's boys – espesially if we duck down when a big one come across. We have names for them, "minnies" and "whizz bangs" or other ruder words. Every time our lot start up I think to myself – if it's one of Maggie's those Huns had better watch out – it will be very high explosive! I told the men and now all the boys in my section nudge each other and say – Hope it's one of Maggie's. Soon we may be moving and then I might not be abel to write a proper letter. It might be just a field card that you get so I'll say goodbye for now.

On the last day of June Captain Bradley read over his own notes taken from the orders for the battalion:

Dawn tomorrow – mines will explode, gun barrage will lift. All along the line the infantry will conduct a measured, considered advance. Necessary for each man to carry full kit as not envisaged that there will be any retreat from the forward positions which will be occupied on the first day of the advance. Our bombardment will have thrown the enemy into turmoil, destroying their defences and disrupting their supplies. Resistance may be encountered beyond the first line of defence, but not before. Led by their Commanding Officer, the soldiers will advance in line formation, walking slowly.

Chapter 16

JOHN MALCOLM STOOD with his fellow soldiers waiting for the signal to go forward. The trenches were full, crushed with the dense pack of men brought up from the rear in readiness for the dawn attack. In front of his battalion were the Royal Inniskilling Fusiliers who were going in as the first wave, and on their right to the rear the men of the Essex's who were to follow after. John Malcolm knew that along mile upon mile of the Front, regiment after regiment of the Army was in a long line ready to engage. They had been told that history would be made today, and he was aware of his own place here with men from Newfoundland and South Africa, from India and Australia and New Zealand, men from Tyneside, Northumbria and Wales. His exhilaration at being part of it ran through his whole being, his mind fired with the words the Corps Commander had addressed to them before the night march from the wood at Acheux. The sense of dislocation that he had experienced on his first tour of duty in the trenches was gone. To begin with, walking in these deep angular fissures of the earth, with the only fixed constant being the narrow running strip of sky above, had made him feel at once remote and insignificant, yet at the same time as if at any moment he could be plucked out and up into the cosmos. All that had now dissipated. This morning he was clearly fixed in time and space, with a deep sense of identity and purpose. He stood with the absolute firmness of spirit that comes with certitude of resolve, his heart singing with confidence.

The bombardment of the previous week meant that there could be little left of the German defences, and they had just heard the sappers' huge mine going off to the north at Hawthorn Redoubt. The Captain's eye was on his watch as the minutes ticked towards 7.30 a.m. As soon as they'd given enough time for the dust to settle, they'd get out and walk forward to mop up any pockets of resistance.

Beside him Eddie Kane swallowed in nervous excitement. 'We're really here! I can hardly believe it. Think of what we're going to tell them when we get back home!'

The whistles for his battalion blew, and laden with his full pack, John Malcolm clambered along the trench line and out through the path marked in their own wire. He struggled to his feet, gripped his rifle firmly with both hands, and walked steadily into the rising sun.

Maggie was hurrying, late for the early morning bus, when she passed the postman on the village main street.

'You have a special one all to yourself,' he said and handed her a letter addressed to her in John Malcolm's handwriting.

Maggie thrust the letter in her coat pocket and forgot about it until break time in the factory, when she found a quiet corner to sit down and read it.

Maggie, my dear sister,

Maggie stared at the words in surprise; it was unlike her brother to use such emotive words.

I'm sending this letter down the line and hope it reaches you safe. The big attack is on. We're going over the top in a few hours, and I wanted to write you in case I don't make it through. For weeks now I've been so worried that when the time came I'd funk it, but they've promised us an extra rum ration, and anyway I'm set in my mind now, so don't worry on that score.

I'd like you to look out for Charlotte. I think she'll take it hard. I never thought of it before, but I suppose soldiering is a selfish thing to do. Here I am having all the excitement, and those at home have the worry and the waiting.

Her last letter said that she met you on the bus and that she enjoyed talking to you. She is such a good and kind person, and I'm sure that if you got to know her better you'd like her a lot. Please try for my sake Maggie. Have to go now. God bless.

your loving brother, John Malcolm

Maggie crushed the letter in her hand. He was going to die. She knew it with blinding certainty. And he knew it too. She felt like running, now, this minute, to find Charlotte. To grasp the younger girl and hold her tight against her own body, to protect her from the terrifying truth. That they would never see him again, and, like so many others, he wasn't coming back, not at all, not ever.

Tim Bradley went down at once with a bullet in his head. The Captain spun back and fell heavily, arms and legs outsplayed. John Malcolm had to swerve to avoid him, but only briefly glanced down. He must keep going as he'd been told to do. It seemed that there was more enemy fire than they'd expected. Many of the Irish had fallen only yards into No Man's Land. Eddie must have gone too, because without turning his head John Malcolm knew that there was no longer anyone beside him. He tried not to think about that, and concentrated on moving forward. But now there were more fallen men in front of him, and he had to walk round or climb over them, as they crawled about on the earth, or lay still upon it. The air sputtered and flicked at his face. He managed another hundred paces before there was a tearing pain in his chest and his legs which slewed him sideways, and he fell face down into a shell-hole.

Maggie looked at the date on John Malcolm's letter: 1 July 1916. She raised her eyes and looked down at the factory floor where the dust and the noise were never-ending. Below her, ranks of shells stood waist high to the men and women who walked among them checking primers on the nose cones. Outside it was midsummer. Here where sunlight could never reach was destruction and death.

John Malcolm's latest letter to Charlotte had caused her to stop and think. It didn't start in her the feeling of absolute terror that his letter to Maggie had done, but it had left her anxious and thoughtful.

Dear Charlie,

Thank you again and again for your little parcels. It is such a good idea to send lots of small packages rather than one big one. The rest of the men are jealous, as at every post delivery I have lots of letters to open. Charlie, you are so sweet and gentle and full of little kindnesses. I am so lucky to have met you, Charlie, and had some time with you.

I wish you could have met our Captain, Tim Bradley. He is a great chap. Yesterday he gathered us about him and told us –

"It's tough work and no mistake, but there's a job to be done. Keep in mind it's for your Ma and Pa, and your little brother and sister, and your sweetheart or child. I want you to know that I'll be leading you out. You'll follow behind me, and I'll be with you every step of the way. You'll walk side by side together, and if some should fall, and make no mistake some will, then those that do will urge the rest on. You're fighting, not for yourself, but for liberty against an oppressor. We are not here for glory, but for freedom, and the bond to buy that is a soldier's life. It may be that you are called upon to pay it. So, I ask you if you go down, then cheer on the man beside you."

Charlie, there wasn't a man without a tear in his eye.

So, Charlie, it may be a while before you hear from me. I know that I am doing the right thing. Here's hoping it all works out and we'll see each other again soon.

much love from me to you, John Malcolm

Charlotte reread the letter, her eye caught by her name, *Charlie*. John Malcolm had written her name five times in his letter. She held the letter against her heart and imagined his voice, pretended to herself that she could hear him speaking the words. His other letters she had read so often that she knew them off by heart. Sometimes she recited parts of them to herself when she was busy in the ward, especially when doing some of the more unpleasant work. It kept her mind off the terrible smell and offensive bandages and made her happy, so that a smile was constant on her face. But this letter troubled her, snagging in her mind from time to time throughout the day.

John Malcolm was aware of being turned over and his field dressing pulled from the pocket in his uniform. He felt someone working on his chest, and then a morphine tablet was slipped under his tongue.

'Good lad,' whispered John Malcolm.

The man laughed. 'Good lad, yourself,' he said.

'Can you get me in?'

'Not at present, son. They're raising merry hell out there.'

'Are we winning?'

The stretcher-bearer looked out beyond the shell-hole where the Irish and the Scots were piled in front of the enemy's uncut wire, and then back to the face of the dying boy. 'We're winning,' he lied.

'All along the line?'

'All along the line.'

The stretcher-bearer had gone. John Malcolm wasn't frightened. They had been told that the wounded might have to wait until nightfall to be brought in. He tried to ease his body round and saw that another soldier had dropped down beside him. He sensed that this man was saying something but his own hearing was dulled, his brain beating in tune with the slow delicious sweep of the morphine.

The man gave him water from his own water bottle. He tried to say 'thank you' but although the thought and its meaning was there before him, the words would not come. Instead he told this soldier how proud he was to be in uniform, and how fighting to protect those at home gave his life a purpose he did not know it had. Time passed, and now John Malcolm knew that there was something he had to say. He struggled against the pressing pain in his chest, and the thickness of his tongue in his mouth. Things were not right. Something very fundamental was wrong: wrong with his body, wrong with the battle, wrong with the world. He didn't know what it was, and when he tried to think about it, his mind moved away, one thought sliding behind another, all of them obscured by some other imminent thing, which when he reached for it was itself obscured. And through all of this, he sought in the labyrinths of his reasoning for the one thing that was right.

And then he had it. John Malcolm smiled. It was suddenly so clear in his head and his mouth. The one shining truth that surpassed all others. He opened his eyes and looked into the light.

'Charlie,' he said softly.

The soldier beside him waited what he considered a decent interval. Then he stretched across, and with his two fingers closed down the boy's eyelids.

The telegram lay on the kitchen table.

Her father sat with his head in his hands, her mother with her arms folded rocking backwards and forwards.

Maggie got to her feet. 'I must go and tell Charlotte.'

As she reached the end of the village she could see a slight figure leaning against the bridge. It was Charlotte, standing with her arms wrapped around herself.

Maggie hesitated. 'Are you waiting for someone?' she asked her.

Charlotte's eyes met hers. 'I am waiting for you,' she said.

Maggie handed her the telegram.

The girl appeared to diminish before her eyes. Shrinking into herself, withdrawing to some other inner place, and then slow tears edged from her eyes and flowed unchecked. Awkwardly Maggie put her arms around her. When Charlotte's tears had eased a little Maggie spoke.

'You knew?'

'I knew that nearly every house in the village had received a telegram. And I knew that if you had received one then you would come this way to tell me.' Her tear-stained face fixed itself on Maggie's. 'How can we bear it?' she wailed. 'What are we going to do?'

Maggie felt her own tears begin. 'I don't know,' she said. 'I don't know.' And she sat down in the road and began to cry.

Chapter 17

ALEX WENT TO the end of the lane behind the shop and sat down with his shoulders against the wall of the wash-house block. If he tried hard he could squeeze tears from the back of his eyes behind his lids, but there wasn't enough to make them run down his face. What was the matter with him?

Why didn't he feel like crying? John Malcolm was gone. His big brother, his only brother, was killed in the War. The person who had looked out for him when he was small and taught him how to box so that none of the street lads could pick on him. John Malcolm had wrestled with him on the drying green, and played chases with him up and down this lane. So why did he not feel more sad?

Perhaps it was because he didn't really believe it. Everybody was acting as though he were dead, but maybe he wasn't. It could be a mistake and John Malcolm might be a prisoner of the Germans. Although that could be worse. There were awful stories about what the Germans did to their prisoners. He'd heard they cut their hands off. Alex looked at his wrists. He didn't fancy his hands being cut off. Better to be shot. He raised his arms as if holding an imaginary rifle and took aim along the lane.

A late shaft of sun struck a path of pale light in front of him. His movements and the rubbing of his clothes against the wall was causing the dust to dance, and casting shadows through the air. Someone was standing there. Alex lowered his arm, his play acting forgotten. A soldier in uniform. Alex screwed up his eyes. The sunlight expanded slowly, and then there was nothing.

A voice spoke behind him. 'You been sent out the house too?'

Alex looked round. It was his friend Hugh Kane. Alex nodded.

'Did your ma get a telegram?'

Alex nodded again.

'Us too. Eddie's dead.'

Alex gulped. He hadn't thought of any others.

'There was lots,' said Hugh. 'Up and down the lanes, lots of doors got chapped this afternoon.'

'How's your ma?' Alex asked Hugh.

'She's gone round to my granny's house. Do you want to come home with me and I'll make some pieces?'

As he got up to follow Hugh, Alex looked back along the lane behind his house. It was empty. All he could see were shadows and sunlight.

They walked through the streets. It was the middle of the day, yet many blinds were drawn down. In Hugh's kitchen there was a black wooden box with brass hinges lying open on the table. Family papers, birth certificates and a few sepia photographs lay vulnerable and exposed.

'She was looking at our photographs.' Hugh pointed to a formal group showing a man in uniform, two very young boys and a woman holding a babe in arms. 'My da was killed in the Boer War when I was a baby, so now there's only me and her.'

Alex looked at the photograph. 'Why are there three children?'

'I had an older brother, Kenneth,' Hugh pointed to the middle child, 'but he died when he was two. Now there's just me left.' He put the photograph back into the box.

Mrs Kane came into the house. Her face was puffed and swollen, but she smiled readily at the boys. Alex couldn't think what to do. He stood up and, copying the actions of the men in his father's shop, he stuck out his hand. 'My condolences,' he said.

Hugh's mother took his hand and covered it with her own. 'And mine to you,' she said. Then she burst into tears.

Alex stared. It was the first time he had seen a grown-up cry openly. A wild panic entered his mind. He hated Germans, all Germans; that they could do this to the people he knew, strip them of their dignity, made him frightened and angry. 'Put the box away for me, Hugh,' she sobbed, 'I can't bear to look at them now.' And she threw her apron over her face and went into the back room.

Alex watched Hugh gather up the photographs and certificates. He stretched his hand out.

'You make your ma a cup of tea, and I'll do that.'

Hugh handed over the box gratefully and went to the range.

'Shall I put it away in the press?' asked Alex.

Hugh nodded.

'I'll just go then?'

Hugh nodded again.

Alex could see that his friend's shoulders were shaking and he guessed that he was crying. He closed the box lid and placed it carefully on the top shelf of the cupboard. 'Right, 'bye.' Alex let himself out of the front door and walked away down the road.

That night Alex reached out in bed for his brother and knew before he awoke that there was no-one there. When John Malcolm had first gone off, Alex had gloried in the extra space he had gained, but now the bed was empty and cold. Where once he had cuddled against his brother's back on bitter winter nights now he would be for ever alone.

In school the next day the head teacher led the children in prayer for those loved ones who had died in the battles near the River Somme. 'This is all you children can do, watch and pray,' he told them.

Alex kept his face still and his eyes looking straight ahead so that no-one would guess his thoughts. He spoke silently to himself. 'No,' he said, 'there is more that I can do.'

A week later Maggie met Francis at the bus stop as she waited for the early morning bus to the city. He was carrying a small suitcase.

'I was very sorry to hear about your brother,' he said gently.

Maggie nodded. She could feel tears in her throat and didn't trust herself to speak. He sat beside her on the journey to the city with his suitcase at his feet.

'How is Charlotte?' she asked him after a while.

'She was very unwell for a few days. But now she is a little better and has returned to work.'

Maggie remembered John Malcolm's last letter to her and was uncomfortable. 'Would company help? I could call at your house if . . .'

Francis turned to her eagerly. 'Oh, that is so kind of you. My mother is possibly not fully aware of how attached my sister was to your brother, and I'm sure that speaking to you would comfort Charlotte. She would appreciate it tremendously, especially when she realizes that I have gone.'

Maggie stared at him and then at the suitcase. 'You haven't told her that you are going away?'

'I left a note,' he said awkwardly. 'I am going to enlist.'

Maggie shook her head in disbelief. 'You cannot do that.' And then, as he did not reply, she asked, 'Who spoke to you that made you change your mind?'

'I have not changed my mind,' said Francis.

'Then why are you going to fight in a war that you believe is wrong?'

'In the circumstances it is the best thing to do—'

Maggie interrupted at once. 'Your sister would never wish you to rush off to war because . . .' her voice broke on her brother's name, . . . John Malcolm has been . . . been killed.'

'It is more complex than that. My mother is terribly upset. Her sister's two boys, my cousins, Connor and Phelan, have also been killed.'

'Perhaps you would be better at home if both your mother and your sister need support?' suggested Maggie.

Francis shook his head. 'I feel that my presence is a constant reminder that others died in vain.'

'You are not taking it upon yourself to complete what they began, surely?' asked Maggie.

Francis gazed at her. 'It is all piled on my head.'

'You mustn't think like that,' said Maggie. 'You cannot accept responsibility for the deaths of others. They didn't die because you weren't there.'

'Do you think that I am driven to do this by feelings of guilt?'

'I don't know what it is that is driving you,' said Maggie. 'What I do know is that you should not do something that you so clearly do not believe in.'

Francis sat in miserable silence for a while.

'You despise me,' he said.

'Oh, no!' cried Maggie.

'In many ways it is a relief,' said Francis. 'To go now and get it over and be done with it.'

Maggie looked at him in alarm. 'It won't be very helpful to the Army,' she said, 'if you have such a careless regard for your own life.'

Francis gave a small laugh. 'You have such a turn of phrase, Maggie. Being "helpful" to the Army is not my prime consideration. I have been in touch with Major Grant, and he says he can secure me a commission in the Queen's Westminster Rifles. He says that every regiment is crying out for officers.'

They sat in silence until the bus reached the outskirts of the city when Francis turned to her and said, 'May I write to you? Don't feel obliged to reply or send anything,' he went on hurriedly. 'It's only that it would be good to have someone to write to with whom I could be open.'

'Please feel free to write to me at any time.'

'Do you mind?' he asked.

'Not at all,' she replied, and then catching sight of the factory gates she rose to go. 'This is my stop.' She held out her hand, and as Francis shook it Maggie found herself unsure as to how to bid him goodbye. She could hardly say 'take care' when he obviously didn't intend to, and to wish him luck seemed absurd. He held her hand quite tightly and it was she who had to disengage herself. She gave a quick incline of her head and hurriedly got off the bus.

Chapter 18

AS SOON AS she was able Maggie went to see Charlotte, so that by the time Francis's first letter arrived she was able to reply that she and Charlotte had talked and had tea together. Charlotte had lost weight, and Maggie felt like a fussy mother hen as she urged her to eat the sandwiches and cakes prepared by Annie. Annie herself hovered around the girls trying to coax Charlotte to try some of her special gingerbread, until eventually Charlotte suggested that she and Maggie go outside and walk in the garden.

'Annie has the best of intentions,' said Charlotte, 'but I hate being fussed over.'

'She is concerned for you,' said Maggie. 'As I am,' she added quite truthfully.

'I am well enough,' Charlotte told Maggie. 'Better than I thought I might be. Our family doctor has given me something to help. But it is difficult, especially at night.'

‘Yes,’ said Maggie, thinking of her own house at night, where she sometimes awoke to the sound of her mother crying. Often her own grief made her unable to sleep and she would lie in the dark remembering her loved and loving brother. ‘I don’t know if it helps to talk . . .’

Charlotte stopped on the path, and clenching her hand she placed it just below the base of her throat. ‘Just here,’ she said, ‘is lodged a large lump of ragged glass. I carry it with me always. It occupies my mind and body. I am conscious of it as I breathe, eat, speak, think. Sometimes it presses so hard within me, I think that my heart might stop.’ She turned her large grey eyes to Maggie. ‘I did not know that grief could take on an actual physical form.’

Maggie went and stood close to the younger girl. Charlotte leaned her head on Maggie’s shoulder. Neither of them cried. Maggie’s own manifestation of grief was stunning numbness. Her own life had become locked into the day of John Malcolm’s last letter, when she had known that he was dead, days before the telegram had arrived.

‘There is a Sister Bateman at the hospital,’ said Charlotte. ‘Her fiancé was killed at Mons. When I first started working in the city hospital she was dreadful to me. Now she is helping me complete my Nursing Certificates.’

'Everyone tries to be kindly,' said Maggie. 'Customers in the shop, my friends in the factory. It is so difficult just to go about and do the things of the day, but I find the activity of demanding work helps.'

'So, we manage,' said Charlotte, 'because we have to.' She took Maggie by the arm as they walked on among the trees where the leaves were already dappling to gold and auburn.

Apart from work and friends, Maggie found relief from her mourning from an unexpected source. When the first short letters arrived from Francis Armstrong-Barnes she had read them quickly and written back from a sense of duty; a promise that she had made and must keep. But as time went on and he completed his officer training and then moved from England to France, she found that she was reading some of his letters more than once, and taking more care with her own replies. She told herself that it was due to the approaching winter and letter writing was something to do by the fire in the dark evenings. His letters had become longer and slightly disjointed, written at different times over several days. She found them thoughtful and interesting, and finally had to acknowledge to herself that she looked forward to receiving them.

Dear Maggie,

France, finally, and then to Belgium and brigade H2. Battle training, lectures, marches, gas attack drill. The main activity appears to have "shut down" for the winter – (as though it were the close of some sporting season). I made this last comment in the Officers' Mess the other night. "Yes, what!" exclaimed one of my fellow officers. "Pity really. I'd hoped to bag a few so that I could write home about it. It's going to be an awful wait until the spring." It took a few seconds before I realized that he'd thought I was serious and was agreeing with me.

This country is beautiful, softer than at home, although we have a greater variety of trees. Here there are pretty fields with bursting hedgerows, and little canals and rivers lined with poplars. Behind the salient is one of Belgium's hop-growing districts and the cane towers supporting the crop make the landscape distinctive.

There are shady areas with willows stooped by the river's edge trailing long branches down into the water. Summer is leaving the land. People speak of the year fading but I've always thought of Autumn as a positive season. Harvest is being gathered in, and although the colours are pigments from a restricted palette, your eye appreciates them the more for having each shade displayed; a spectrum spanning palest yellow to burnt umber. This evening the sky itself is old gold with flashes from the barrage cracking along the horizon.

Now going forward to our battalion billets – can one ever become accustomed to the sound of gunfire? The countryside that we now march through is scarred with the debris of war, ammunition dumps, huge piles of empty shell cases. Trees are being felled by the hundred for fuel and army supplies, shelter for horses and men. The annihilation of the woods makes the land bleak, and grimmer still are the makeshift cemeteries with rows and rows of wooden crosses. Every village and hamlet we march through the people come out to see us. Children run with little flowers they have picked from the roadside. Women, even the young, wear mainly black. Many are dressed in traditional costume with wooden clogs. They stop working in the fields and call out as we pass.

Now at billet, and our draft has been added to the regulars – very depleted after their engagements around Bapaume. Our soldiers seem still quite resolute and most manage to stay cheerful in appalling circumstances. They fill me with hope, and amaze me. The ones I've spoken to who have been in the front line are weary with bloodshot eyes. We can only imagine what they've been through.

Yours,

Francis Armstrong-Barnes

He had added at the end:

Soon we won't have to imagine.

To begin with Maggie had no idea what to write in reply. Francis did not ask for anything, neither home news nor items to be sent, so in her first letters she confined herself to comments about the weather. But as Francis's letters arrived from abroad they seemed to need more, demand an attention that was almost personal. She had an inkling of how much their correspondence meant to him by one letter she received.

It is a sobering moment when the post arrives. Each man withdraws to some quiet place and each gives the other a little space and privacy for the news from home is not always welcome or good. What cuts a chap up above all else is if he gets word that his sweetheart, or wife indeed, has found someone else. It seems such a betrayal to them when they are suffering so much deprivation and daily bombardment.

We live daily with death so that hearing of another's elsewhere is not such a blow as I expect it is at home. Although occasionally a low groan will alert you to the fact that some poor chap has been told that this brother or best friend has been killed. It might have happened many months ago, only a few miles from our own sector, yet this is their first news of it. Time and space seem strangely disjointed that this news should travel all the way from Belgium to Britain, and then from Britain back here again.

They are undertaking searches of the battlefields on ground we have gained, trying to locate men who have been killed in earlier engagements. I only write this so that you will know that this unpleasant but necessary work is being organized and annotated, and I feel sure that your family will learn in time where John Malcolm is buried. I know that it is a heartache for relatives not to know where their loved ones lie. I think often of Annie's two boys, and there is, of course, the writer Rudyard Kipling's son, who went missing at Loos in 1915. They say that this experience has made him become involved with this work. The great loss he has suffered must surely affect his soul as a writer. You will have read his work.

Maggie looked at the last sentence, *You will have read his work.* Francis obviously had read Kipling, and assumed that she had too. But she hadn't. There was little time for her to read books, and not much point either, unless it was a recipe or an account. She had been destined to work in the shop until she married. Now she knew that she had missed out in some way and her lack of knowledge meant that she could not adequately respond to Francis.

There was a library in Springbank close to the munitions works. After work the next day Maggie crossed the road and went inside. It was the first time she had been in a public library. She cautiously asked for anything by Rudyard Kipling, and was given two books. It seemed frivolous to be reading fiction at all and even more so reading poetry. But now she was more content, she could write back to Francis telling him that she had borrowed from the public library and very soon she would send him her comments on Kipling's work.

Chapter 19

ONE NIGHT IN October when dinner had been eaten, Maggie cleared and washed up and then sat down at the kitchen table with pen and paper before her. A letter had come from Francis that morning, and she needed to think carefully before she replied. He was now on a second tour of duty at the Front and enduring all the hardship involved in active service there. She thought of one of her brother's last letters home, where John Malcolm had cheerily talked about the lice which appeared to be endemic.

> *. . . They are absolutely everywhere, I am covered in blotchy red bites. Ma would have fourteen fits. The old stagers take off their shirts and run a lit match along the seams. You can hear the bugs craking as they're burnt, and the men say it gives them a bit of peace from the bites for a while. The lice give off a strange smel, a stalenes which clings to your clothes, but I have to tell you truthfully you very soon get used to it.*

He had added at the end:

What can't be cured must be endured . . .

This last sentence was a saying her mother and father used frequently. Maggie recognized it, and when she read it she at once knew her brother's state of mind. Reading Francis's letters was always more challenging. She sometimes struggled to grasp his thoughts as he had put them on paper. Occasionally they contained references that she did not fully understand. But although it gave her difficulty, she felt pleased that he wrote to her in this way, neither watering down his experiences, nor addressing her as a child, the way men frequently did to women. Letters from Francis took longer to get through and it helped to read them more than once, yet she found them all the more satisfying because of that. The letter she had received today made grim reading. It did not begin 'Dear Maggie' but with a quote which Maggie recognized from *Macbeth,* a play her teacher had read with them in her last year at school.

"O Horror! Horror! Horror! Tongue nor heart cannot conceive nor name thee!"

I had to lead a sortie out into No Man's Land the other night. We had left it very late as we knew that the other lot had been out and about earlier. They had come off rather the worst in the last engagement with their front line taking a pounding, and some oaf in command on their side (no doubt wanting to buck them up a bit) had sent them over to try to flush out our sector. We had beaten them back (just) but a lot of their chaps were badly wounded and were lying where they'd fallen, or had crawled for shelter into shell-holes. It's the decent thing to do (they do it for us) to let them try to get to their wounded, either to bring them back in or sort them out – this is a charming euphemism for despatching any poor chap taking too long to die, which is a mercy really and I hope someone takes as much care for me if required. The rats rush for raw flesh, and don't care whether it's live or dead. These vermin are fat-bellied and full and scurry about their business quite fearlessly.

At this point Maggie had to stop reading. She took her handkerchief from her pocket and held it to her mouth.

It was about daybreak, with that strange dawn appearing as it does on this flat land below sea level with no hills to reflect or filter the early sun. We had done all that was needed and I was crawling back to our lines when a starlight shell went up and I quickly lay flat, arms flung out. One of my outstretched hands connected with metal. I had a quick looksee and it was a magnificent Prussian helmet. When the flare faded I slowly pulled the helmet towards me. I have no interest in souvenirs, but others do, and back at billet it would be worth a few fresh eggs or some fruit. I got it to within an inch of my face when I was aware of squealing sounds and claws scrabbling on my hand. I felt movement between my fingers. And then in the half dark my eyes could see that the helmet was still attached to a human skull with putrid flesh clinging in parts, and a rat had made its nest within. Scuttling through the eye sockets and crawling on my hand and arm were the blind offspring of this evil vermin. With a great cry I threw the whole thing from me and lay there shaking.

On reflection, what should please me about this particular rat is the fellow's impartiality. He had chosen a German skull to set up home, yet had wisely decided to plunder British uniform to line its nest, no doubt aware of the superior quality of the cloth. I recognized the three stripes of a sergeant on a piece of khaki – unfortunately there was still part of the sergeant adhering to it. A wise rat indeed. It had found food, and a shelter for its brood to protect them from the bitter winds which blow across this devastated land.

I was unable to do as much, for on return from the sortie I had a bit of a set-to with my Commanding Officer. The troops have burrowed little nooks for themselves in against the trench wall. These are known as "funk holes" and the men take turns to huddle down and try to get a bit of shut-eye when not on duty. And they are as brave a bunch of lads as you could wish to meet, and without them I would be quite gone in the head by now. But the nights are becoming bitter, and when one is allowed an hour or two's sleep it is difficult to sleep with legs and feet encased in mud-frozen puttees. I went to my C.O. to request an extra blanket or two for the men in the front line trenches. He turned me down.

"It wouldn't do," he said.

He explained why. Maggie, if you can, appreciate the irony of this. I was informed that those of us in command must positively discourage the men from making themselves too comfortable, as it might make them want to remain where they are. Any fitment which looks as though it might be of a permanent nature is to be frowned upon.

"We have to convince the men that we soon will move forward," he said, "that the trenches are a temporary accommodation only."

I said, "But Sir, we have occupied these very same trenches for the last two years. The men cannot have failed to notice this."

To which he replied:

"Nevertheless."

I found myself unable to respond. In the face of such monumental madness, my chin began to shake and I could not articulate a reply.

He stared at me with his pale eyes. I had never noticed before quite how pale his eyes and lashes are.

Then he said, "You may go."

Maggie, I had thought that at home we were being deluded by false tales, that we were prevented from hearing what was actually going on at the Front. It would appear that the delusion is widespread. Perhaps it is only the soldier who stares out from the firestep who can actually see what is there. I have stood with that soldier.

I am with a couple of them now, occupying a forward position in the sap trench looking out across this bleak God-cursed wasteland. And bleak it is, and cursed it must be, Maggie. What great wrong did humanity commit that we suffer thus? In what way did we offend the gods that they choose to take their revenge in such a manner? We must cry to heaven to be forgiven.

The letter was unsigned as though Francis had been unable to continue.

Along the bottom he had scrawled:

But can we ever forgive ourselves?

Maggie read and reread the letter. It needed a reply, and quickly. Francis's way of writing out this black tragedy had overtones of despair which frightened her. The intensity and mocking humour reverberated within her. She was utterly convinced that he wrote to no-one else like this, and she knew therefore that she must take great care with her reply. This man would not be fobbed off with any easy form of words, consoled with trite remarks. If she wrote to him in that manner it might only serve to deepen his isolation. She had started her letter two or three times before she concluded there were no comforting words that she could give him, for there was no comfort at all to be given.

The only thing to do was to write the truth. Maggie took a fresh piece of paper, picked up her pen and began again.

Francis, the things you see and hear each day are truly terrible and all I can write back to you is of the things I see and hear each day, which are plain and of little import.

But perhaps they will serve to take your mind off your own troubles for a space of time.

The girls in the munitions factory talk mostly of young men, of fashions and of style. At the start of each new week several more heads have been bobbed, as the weekend is when we have a little free time and the girls are becoming more skilled and daring with the hair shears. The reason given is that long hair is dangerous and, despite wearing our head caps, it could get caught in the machinery, but the truth is that men whistle at a girl with bobbed hair. And although a girl must always appear offended when this happens and threaten to report the man concerned, it would be most dreadful if one never collected a single whistle. As you can see our most dreadful experience differs from yours.

Fashion too occupies a great deal of our thoughts. How far up should a hem go? It has now been accepted generally that ankles should be on display. But is it attractive to reveal anything above the ankle? Would more be vulgar? Someone returned from a visit to London not so long ago saying that ladies were showing three inches in the Strand. There is a girl in the factory called Mabel who operates one of the slot-drilling machines, and her cousin spoke to a neighbour whose husband was on leave in Paris recently. Mabel has let us know that her cousin told her that this neighbour's husband wrote to her from Paris to say that he saw a young woman on a bicycle there who was showing her knees. This was thought to be going too far, even for the French. However it was pointed out that the girl was cycling at the time, and also that there is probably a shortage of dressmaking cloth in Paris, so the circumstances are different. But how much can a man cope with? We all agree that there is a line to be drawn between attracting and teasing. Can a girl stay respectable when doing this? Your advice on this matter would be appreciated.

Our greatest battle has been over the use of the lavatory. The female munitions workers have been accused of using their time there to gossip, and a move has been made to reduce lavatory usage. Regular habits are to be encouraged by employing a reward system for infrequent use. I am sure you do not need me to tell you the indignation and outrage this has caused among the girls. It was decided at once that we would not tolerate these indelicate accusations, and that we would resist such unjust action. It may be that our visits there are more frequent and take a little longer time, but that is only to be expected. We have objected to this attack on our territory. Negotiations about a rota system are taking place, but rest assured, like plucky little Belgium, we will stand firm!

Then, without any deliberation on her part, rather than writing 'Maggie Dundas' as she had done in her previous letters, Maggie signed this letter 'Maggie'.

A week later she received her reply.

Maggie, my dear friend,

We received our mail yesterday and I am writing back at once so that you will know how much good your letter has done for us here. What a tonic! What a boost to morale! I had to wipe tears from my eyes I laughed so much. And my laughter was so loud that my men pestered me incessantly to tell them why I was laughing, and, Maggie, I hope you don't mind too much, but I was compelled to read your letter out to them. It had such a reception that I have now read it aloud to various groups six or seven times or more.

There is much argument here about what is respectable and what is not, and what a good gel should or should not do regarding hemlines. I have to report that the general opinion of a soldier looking forward to leave after many months at the Front is that a hemline should go up as far as possible, and that the more unrespectable the girl the better. The proviso being, of course, that one's own wife/sweetheart should not occupy this category.

The Battle of the Lavatory caused much amusement, as here on occasion (and I hope this does not disgust you too much) one's helmet, or an empty corned beef tin can be pressed into service. However, you will be pleased to know that the men support the women munitions workers. A call to arms was issued and every soldier volunteered for duty. They have formed the 1st Latrine Brigade, raised colours, and intend to apply to the Colonel for transfer to duty on this new important Front.

Regarding length of hair, the argument rages on. Long hair is winning – bad news for the bobs! However, if having one's hair cut short means that the munitions girls do not have to wear the headcoverings designed to keep their hair out of the machinery, then we favour the bob, as this platoon, to a man, does not like viewing a young woman's head wrapped up like a dumpling. (A pretty hat being an entirely different matter.)

You will appreciate that I have had to censor many of the remarks, but let me say that these discussions have caused merriment up and down the line. My stock among the men has gone up tremendously. I am offered cigarettes as I pass by. The whole battalion is grateful to you. I have asked the Major to recommend you to be decorated. The King will write to you shortly.

Francis

Along the bottom of the letter Francis had written a PS:

Maggie, this is by far the best letter I have ever received. It came at a moment when I was very low and has quite restored me.

In the factory all that day Maggie had a smile on her face.

Chapter 20

CHARLOTTE, ON MAGGIE'S insistence, had taken to calling in at the shop on her way home from the hospital. Maggie had told her that it would be good for her parents to see Charlotte and speak with her, although Charlotte rightly suspected that Maggie's purpose was also to help *her.* Whether her visits helped John Malcolm's parents was something Charlotte could not clearly assess. His mother's pain of loss was burnt into her face. She was abstracted, and found it difficult to keep her place in any conversation that she attempted. His father, in tight control, would say a few words and then keep himself busy in the shop long after closing. It was Maggie and Alex that Charlotte saw most, and talking to them did help her pass some of the bleak time of each weary evening to be endured. She became friendly with Alex, and was forever patient with his endless questions about her work at the hospital. He wanted to know every single thing that the soldiers said to her, and gave her lists of questions to ask them on his behalf, telling her it was special schoolwork that he had to do. The wounded men were amused by this, and, as hospital life was boring for them, were quite willing to write out notes which Charlotte relayed back to Alex. He had asked her for anything of interest, and she, thinking he had thoughts of becoming a doctor, brought him one of the small surgical information books relating to war wounds.

Alex had no intention of studying medicine. He was methodically garnering every scrap of information that might be of use to him in avenging the death of his brother. After he had gone to bed one night Maggie picked up from the kitchen table the book on treating war wounds.

Treating war wounds needs an elementary knowledge of the agents which cause them, she read, *rifle, revolver, machine gun, shell, trench mortar, bombs and grenades.* Her eye ran down the page . . . *Shell wounds in particular cause great damage. Clothing, equipment and earth can be driven deep into the body, causing complications of infection spreading from the wound. Farming soil in particular bears organisms, thereby increasing the chance of severe sepsis leading to fatality.*

Maggie put the book down and stared ahead. It was something that she had not considered at any length. The actuality of death in war. Here it was, carefully explained, cause and effect. *A bullet travelling faster than the velocity of sound, over distance does not always offer a clean drilled hole. Complications of wounds occur as the missile can turn in the air, ricochet, strike bone . . .*

The truth of the words allowed no contradiction, needed no embellishment. To tell in this plain way the violence of the act showed it as the obscenity it was.

This book with its graphic illustrations of mutilated bodies and the effects of gas gangrene had a profound effect on Maggie. She had an image in her mind of the despatch depot in the factory where rows and rows of sullen shells stood awaiting shipment abroad. She thought for a time about the medical facts placed before her, and then she thought of the consequences to herself of having acquired this knowledge. She wished perhaps that she had not read Charlotte's book, but she had, and now she knew that she must alter her life.

She wrote to Francis.

Dear Francis,

I have decided to leave the munitions factory. I cannot work there any longer making instruments of death. I feel that if I at least stop making them then there will be a little less killing. I know that mine is a perverse logic, as it is argued that the more we make the quicker the war would be over. My thought is, that if the manufacturing of arms for the war ceased then there would be no more war. I am sure the mothers and sisters of German soldiers would agree. If this happened, and production everywhere stopped, then so would the war, and the leaders would be forced to conduct a peace. I feel that an overwhelming truth has been revealed to me and I should proclaim it everywhere.

My father is furious with me. The money I earned was very good, but this is only one of the reasons that he is angry. He tells me that it is quite wrong of me to think this way. I do not know how to change this. Can one help what one thinks? I cannot. And should I not be able to express my thoughts the way I want to? Is it because I am a woman that I am restricted in doing this? And that brings me to another reason that he is displeased with me. It is because I thought about it, made the decision, acted, and then told him. To me it seemed the more natural and simpler thing to do. When I first joined in munitions work, I told him in advance and had to conduct endless arguments with him to justify it. This new method seems the best approach. I did feel a little scared in doing it, but also quite exhilarated. I intend to work in the hospital. When I told him this he quietened down a little, and he said that it was a worthy thing to do. And I was glad that he was more content, but I would not have changed my course of action even if he had not been pleased. I am unhappy that I upset my father, but am set now to determine my own course in life.

I read over this letter and I am aware that it is made up of many questions. However, I am not scoring any of it out. Answering them might help exercise your brain and take your mind from other things.

Maggie was surprised by the answer she received from Francis.

Whew! Maggie. What a tart little sentence at the end of your last letter! You should consider becoming a schoolmistress. I am glad that you are out of the factory as it did sound hard and soul-destroying work. I'll consider it an advantage having a nurse as a friend; you can give me any medical advice I may need! The questions you pose in your letter are those that occupy my mind a great deal of the time. Unfortunately here the penalty for promoting such ideas or even discussing such things could be a permanent one. You may remember my father's cousin's strong advice around the time of my visit to his offices in Edinburgh. I met you on the journey home; we took the bus together. I now pass that advice to you.

Maggie frowned and reread this paragraph. Francis was being very guarded in what he was saying, no doubt for fear of the military censor. Why should he be frightened now when his own letters contained such open criticism? Why would he be so concerned? She remembered him talking about the Military Tribunal that had refused his exemption. His father's cousin had told him that his reasoning was dangerous. What did that have to do with her?

His letter went on.

It breaks my heart to say this, but I am going to "lose" your letter. It breaks my heart, as I have every one of the other safe, and read them often as they cheer me up enormously. But this one is a nineteen shillings and seven pence one, or rather, it is not.

Maggie read and reread this part of the letter but could make no sense of it. She glanced up to where Alex sat at the kitchen table doing his homework. Her younger brother was quicker to learn than her twin had been. John Malcolm had struggled with his schoolwork, and had often copied from Maggie so that he could finish quickly and run out to play with his friends. Maggie, who had only helping her mother with housework to look forward to, had always taken longer with her school homework and made more effort. Even in childhood there was injustice within one's own family, Maggie thought. She gave Francis's letter to Alex.

'You are good at puzzles. Solve this one for me, for I can make neither head nor tail of it.'

Maggie sat down at the table with her younger brother. Not so young, she realized as she watched him read the letter. He had grown in the last months, and had the beginnings of hair on his face.

Alex read the letter and then began to count with his pencil marking the lines. 'Safe,' he said, and he underlined the word Francis had written.

'What?' Maggie came across and leaned over Alex's shoulder.

'He's pointing out the word "safe" to you. Lots of soldiers send coded messages in their letters. They sometimes use it to let their families know whereabouts in France they are.'

'Show me,' said Maggie.

'The bit that doesn't make sense is the clue. At the end he says a "nineteen shillings and seven pence, or rather not". If you count nineteen lines down and seven words across then you come to the word "safe". And then he says "or rather, not". So what you wrote in your last letter wasn't safe.'

'But he writes quite openly to me,' said Maggie. 'Why is he concerned about what I write to him?'

'Officers are trusted to censor their own mail,' said Alex. 'Some even have special coloured envelopes which are not opened. But the mail he receives might be inspected before it reaches him.' He looked at Maggie curiously. 'What did you write?'

Maggie picked up Francis's letter. 'Nothing much,' she said. Her hand shook slightly as she folded the letter and put it in her apron pocket. She knew why Francis was concerned for her, and why he was going to destroy the letter she had sent him. What she had written could be considered treason.

Alex waited until Maggie sat down again by the fire before he bent his head over his own work. He carefully slid his school exercise book to the side. Underneath he had a sheet of paper where he had traced a map of England showing the main east coast railway line to London. On it he was marking the headquarters of different army regiments. He had obtained the information via Charlotte from her various soldier patients. 'Careful planning is the key to success.' His brother had written to him that his training sergeant had told him this. Alex intended to plan very carefully indeed. He knew that he must avoid London. It would be the first place they would look for him. Every policeman and army officer would be on the alert. He needed a regimental recruiting office in or near a town with a railway station. It would have to be fairly big, busy and crowded with people so that a person on his own would not be noticed. His finger traced the line of the railway from Edinburgh to London; along the coast, over the border and then the big towns, Newcastle, Durham, Darlington, York, Doncaster, Peterborough . . . He spread out the notes that Charlotte had brought back from the hospital. On them the soldiers had written their answers to his questions. Alex kept one finger on his map. Now he had to match one of these towns to a regiment with a particular type of battalion.

Chapter 21

Dear Maggie,

One of your last letters says that you are borrowing from a library. There are hundreds of books at Stratharden House. You must go at once to my home and speak to my mother, and then begin to use the library there. My father's collection of books has lots of interesting items. Think of it as doing me a favour. I can recommend and you can read, and then we can have famous discussions. If this war ever ends, you can make my letters public, and undertake literary tours giving readings around the Empire and the United States of America. This will make you very famous. As I undoubtedly will be killed, you could wear suitably elegant mourning clothes. Please choose purple rather than black. Black can be drab. Purple is more Royal, and I believe would suit your colouring better. I for my part, will endeavour to raise the standard of my letter writing. Henceforth, so that they may be worthy of publication, they will contain fabulous prose and sound advice – like Lord Chesterfield's letters to his son.

Yours,

Francis

Maggie pencilled a question mark beside *Lord Chesterfield's letters*. She had begun to make little notes on Francis's letters to indicate points to look up in the library. She had no intention of troubling Francis's mother, and on her next visit to the city library she asked the librarian if Lord Chesterfield's letters had been published. He knew of the book but did not have it in stock and suggested she try a bookshop nearer the city centre.

On the bus home Maggie sat in a state of curious delight and fear. Using money from her wages, without first giving them to her mother or father, and then waiting to receive some allowance from them, she had bought something in her own right as a person. And it was not a necessity, such as a hat or shoes, nor even a luxury item like butter or sugar. When she returned home, for some reason she felt that she should not openly read the book she had purchased in front of her parents.

My dear friend Maggie,

It is the most bizarre situation. When I was at home I always felt that we were not being told the half of it or only "through a glass, darkly". Truths, half-truths and lies, but here at the Front we know even less. There are parts of No Man's Land which can only be yards wide. I have a compulsion to shout across and ask them if they have any idea about what is happening. We captured a machine-gunner the other night. We had killed his friend and this chap was seriously wounded. My men carried him in, dressed his wounds, and gave him water from their own water bottles. I cannot make sense of any of it. The one sure and certain belief that I have is that neither does the Allied High Command. Somewhere, we hope, there are a few who possibly have the vestiges of a plan, and they may yet save us all. Meanwhile there is nothing to be done but carry out orders and fill out reports.

Francis

Maggie read the letter again. As with all of Francis's letters there were words she had never seen before. She placed her finger under one of them, *vestiges*. From the rest of the sentence she thought she knew what it might mean. She went to the press in the kitchen where the family's collection of a few books were kept. The basic spelling and grammars that Alex still used didn't help. Maggie resolved that she would visit the bookshop again, and buy herself a proper dictionary.

*

Maggie wrote back,

Dear Francis,

In your last letter you describe one of your men giving the enemy soldier water after taking the German machine-gun post. And then you ask me, "Where is the sense in it all?" It would seem to me that the act of the British soldier in giving the German soldier his water is the one thing that does make sense. A simple gesture of kindness to a fellow human being is the most sensible act I know. Surely it is on this that our existence is based? And if it is not, what is the point of it?

How confidently she could talk of humanity now. Over the last week or so her life had completely altered, both mentally and physically. It was as though she had stepped from behind a curtain, and the world she now occupied was so far removed from her previous one as to make the former unrecognizable. She devoured the books that both Francis and the librarian recommended: biographies, history, travel, letters, fiction, classical and contemporary. She read them on her journey to and from the hospital. Any idea she might have had that nursing would be easier than the munitions factory was soon dispelled. The wards were busy all day. The wounded now arrived via a single line track which had been laid so that trains could bring them directly to a railhead in the hospital grounds. The staff told her things were easing off, as the major battles had been fought in the summer. How ashamed Maggie felt now of her condescending manner to Charlotte in the past. Only those who nursed the seriously ill, the horribly wounded and the dying could know what suffering meant. The effects of unquenchable pain, of gas, of gangrene, and shell shock, made men piteous and pitiable creatures.

'Why did you not ever speak to any of us of this before?' she asked Charlotte.

'Why give others your own burden to carry?'

'They say, "A trouble shared is a trouble halved",' said Maggie.

'Do you believe that, in these circumstances?' asked Charlotte. 'How could I tell Annie or my mother any of this?'

Maggie thought of her own family at home. How her mother or her father would react if she came home and cried out as to how awful it was to change the dressings on a nineteen-year-old boy burned to raw flesh from forehead to feet. 'Yes,' she said. 'I see.' Her experiences, and those of Charlotte and many of the other nurses, women from differing backgrounds, had distanced them from their own families.

But in addition to Charlotte and the other nurses, there was one person whom Maggie could speak to openly. And it was now that she imagined she experienced a little of what

Francis felt in writing to her. To have someone that you could be honest with, a person to tell of your fears and nightmares, brought comfort and release. She wrote of this in her next letter to Francis and he wrote back at once.

I'm so glad that you tell me all this, Maggie. I feel now that I repay some of your enormous kindness in listening to my mad ramblings. I am reserved in my confidences with others here. One senses that everyone else is too, and for the same reason – afraid to become attached too closely and then have to suffer the deprivation that the death of a friend can bring.

My men would make you weep with pride; some are rascally bandits, some malingerers and weak, but all of them have pity for these people who have been brought so low. Villages have disappeared, towns reduced to rubble, their farmland desolated. If you have tears to shed, shed them now for this stricken soil of Belgium. Winter has leeched the colour from the countryside, and man has joined forces to proclaim death to all things. The landscape resembles a radiographic photograph, purged of life, devoid of hope. The nightmarish figures, the blackened tree stumps set against the sky, shell-holes rimed with frost remind of Goya at his most tortuous. I can write and tell you this and it sustains me enough to continue.

This is friendship at its truest, is it not?

Chapter 22

IN EARLY DECEMBER Maggie received a note from Mrs Armstrong-Barnes.

My son writes to say that he wishes you to have access to his library.

He mentions in his letters home that the words you write are of comfort to him. Please allow me to repay this debt of gratitude by calling at Stratharden House for tea this Sunday afternoon.

Maggie found the afternoon less of a chore than she had expected. Mrs Armstrong-Barnes strove to make her welcome, asking her questions about her work at the hospital and in the munitions factory.

'There was an article in the newspaper recently about some titled lady who is most skilled in working a lathe.'

'People from all walks of life work in the munitions factory,' Maggie replied politely. 'Everyone seems to want to help with war work. Charlotte says that you and your friends host charity teas.'

'I don't mind that so much. It means one can make a small contribution.' Mrs Armstrong-Barnes lifted the teapot. 'The War has brought many changes, but actually it's the flowers I miss the most. The gardener would send the boy to the house every week with great armfuls of blooms he had picked, and one of the parlour maids would arrange them. Agnes had such a light touch. Even on the bleakest days she made something of evergreen. The gardener's lad has been called up, and Agnes drives a tram in Liverpool now.' She sighed as she poured the tea. 'Things will never be the same again.' She looked keenly at Maggie. 'But then perhaps you believe that they shouldn't ever be?'

Maggie waited. An answer seemed expected of her, and she considered whether she should oblige or not, finally deciding that to say nothing was in some way wrong. She looked directly at Charlotte's mother. 'I don't think life should be lived the same way as before the War. It is wrong that children go hungry, and I believe that inequality of man and woman is unfair.'

Mrs Armstrong-Barnes gazed out of the window for a moment. 'I know that I should be much more concerned about politics, but I always left that to my husband. He worked so very hard, and my place was to see to the things that enhanced life. Now some of these matters seem so . . . inappropriate.' She stood up. 'I'll leave you to explore the library. Please take whatever interests you, or stay and read here if it is more convenient.'

Maggie had no idea where to begin. She guessed that the books were kept in some kind of order, but in the public library the librarian usually brought her books to her. She set aside a volume of poetry, and then noticed some books on art and artists. Maggie recalled that Francis had visited Europe before the War and studied art subjects at University. She opened one on Goya. He was the Spanish artist Francis had mentioned in one of his letters. The painter, the book said, forsook depicting battle scenes as celebrations of men at war as he began to see these highly stylized representations of glorious victories as propaganda tools. Goya's drawings personalized the conflict of the Spanish Peninsular War, showing individuals maimed, and, importantly for the first time, the horrendous effect of war on a civilian population. The violent twisted shapes assaulted Maggie's eyes and then some extracts from his letters caught her attention, '*. . . in Nature, colour does not exist any more than lines . . . there is only light and shadow . . . relief and depth . . . planes which* *advance and recede . . . Give me a piece of charcoal and I will make you a picture.'*

Goya had used rich colours and a variety of tones in his paintings of Spanish court life, and had then developed the tortuous dark drawings and etchings depicting war. His use of drawing material bonded so well with his chosen subject that they became one force in expressing the horrors of war.

It seemed to Maggie a reflection of Francis's letters, moving from summer in France and Belgium, through autumn, into winter. And, as she read more about Goya, his work and his life, the comparison was more apt, and she knew that she more deeply appreciated the development of Francis's mind and mood. Across the years the artist spoke to her. '*There are no rules in painting . . . it is a deep play of understanding that is needed.*'

Was this how Art fulfilled both creator and receiver? she wondered. Through literature and painting or any other medium; reflecting life, giving vent to emotion, articulating thought, expressing that which could not be encompassed. She felt as though she was on the brink of understanding some great truth, and hurried home carrying the books with her.

Maggie thought that she should explain the gift which she sent Francis with her next letter.

Dear Francis,

I looked at a book on Goya in your library. I have thought about artists and their work. Did Goya need to do this? Why would he torture himself and others with these cruel images of conflict? Was this his way of expressing his liberal sympathies, his hatred of war and oppression? And did he wish to call the attention of others to injustice? Does this then mean that Art can alter opinion and therefore influence future events? I do not know. I do not understand the artistic temperament, and I am afraid that I may have done the wrong thing in sending you this sketch-book and chalks. Does it increase horror to portray it? Does it relieve it? I will not be offended if you trade this gift for some eggs.

It was almost two weeks before Maggie received a communication from Francis. It was a small package and as she unwrapped it she realized it was a page from the sketch-book, wrapped and protected as best he could. It was a drawing of wild flowers, clumps of cornflower and daisy among a cascade of ammunition boxes. Francis had written:

By the side of the trenches, struggling in the fields, and along the parapets, grow mustard seed, and camomile, and poppies. This is such a cathartic gift to give me, Maggie. If the drawing is smudged, it is because I have wept over it.

Maggie kept the drawing by her bedside. Her correspondence with Francis had triggered a reaction within her. Sometimes his letters confused her, with their random mixture of opinion coupled with acute factual observations. His dry comments on his fellow soldiers' behaviour, his deep empathy with the suffering of the French and Belgians, gave her insight into his character. In return, her own writing contained thoughts and emotions such as she never would have expressed under ordinary circumstances. Although at times almost overwhelming her, his letters never failed to stimulate. She resolutely sought to fully comprehend what he was trying to say. Looking up words in her dictionary, pursuing references in the bookshop and library, she enjoyed these quests in themselves, and then when successfully piecing everything together, she would reread his letter and be elated for days.

Was it to do with education? she asked herself. Would she have felt like this had she continued with her schooling at fourteen or fifteen? But learning at school had been functional. Girls were taught to sew and knit, as that would be useful to them in later life. Children learned to count, subtract and do long division with endless combinations of pounds, shillings and pence, so that they could housekeep. Spelling and poems were learned by rote; their words caught and trapped, rather than absorbed and explored. But in his letters Francis wrote about the *meaning* of things; why a thing should be, and why it might not. He challenged opinion (including his own), he discussed creative thought. She had quite simply never experienced anything like this before.

The culmination of all this was that, as Maggie sat one night attempting to reply to Francis's latest letter, she experienced a moment of self-realization. She was sitting in quiet reflection before beginning to write, when she was suddenly conscious of her mind moving. Her thoughts raced away from her in complex patterns. She was on the point of stepping off a ledge, and she found herself trembling.

She wanted to write and tell Francis all of this, but felt inept. She believed that her words might be inadequate, her sentences clumsy. She put her pen down and, holding her hands out in front of her, stared at the fingers that would have to write the words. For a few moments she gazed at her hands, and then slowly she turned them face up. She studied the lines on her palms, some distinct, some interconnecting, small and long, some straight, others arcing, curving in different directions, crosshatching and interlacing, yet each sulcus unique in its own form. Maggie cupped her hands together and put them to her breast.

Chapter 23

IN LATE NOVEMBER Charlotte turned to Maggie in the nurses' rest room at the hospital and said, 'I'm going to France.'

'France!' Maggie repeated. 'Why? Don't you think that you do enough here?'

'No,' replied Charlotte. 'We think that we are working hard, but I have friends who are nursing in the hospitals in France, and they are telling me that more staff are needed. There will be another Offensive in the spring and their situation will worsen.'

'You would leave your mother?'

'My mother has spoken of spending time with her sister since her two boys were killed. She has said that she might let the Red Cross use the house as a convalescent home. My leaving will give her the opportunity to do both.'

'I think your mother thought that you might then take a nursing position within the house,' said Maggie. 'She sees how strained you are, and wants to make things easier for you.'

'I don't want things to be easier. And I could not bear another Christmas and New Year at home.'

'They won't take you when they find out that you are only sixteen,' said Maggie.

'Then I shan't tell them.'

'They'll ask for your birth certificate,' said Maggie. 'There has been such an outcry from mothers about the Army accepting underage recruits that they're bound to check.'

'I have thought about it,' said Charlotte. She picked up a pencil and found a scrap of paper. 'Look, my birth year is 1900. I can easily change it to look like 1896.' She wrote down 1900, and then with a bold stroke she wrote over the number, making it larger and changing the nine to an eight and then the two zeros to a nine and a six. 'See! Now I am twenty!'

'What will your mother say?' Maggie spoke slowly. An idea was beginning to form in her own head. If Charlotte could change her birth certificate, then so could she.

'I'll tell her only that I'm going away to London for special nursing training, which I will have to do in order to qualify to go abroad. She will have to write a letter giving permission for this, but I will dictate the words and make them general enough to cover my nursing abroad. Then by the time I am in France it will be too late for her to do anything about it.'

Maggie leaned over and peered into Charlotte's face. 'You *might* get away with it,' she said. 'You are tall enough . . .' She took Charlotte's chin in her hand and turned her face towards the window, seeing as she did so that pain and grief had wearied her youthful looks. 'If you altered your hairstyle a little, and put on some face powder . . .' Maggie paused. 'If they would accept a probationer, would you mind if I came along?'

'Oh,' said Charlotte. 'I wouldn't mind at all. I'd so appreciate your company. Two friends of mine from the Cottage Hospital are there at the moment.' She laughed. 'They write and tell me about handsome doctors and dashing army officers.'

'And I thought that your main reason was to be like Florence Nightingale.' Maggie struck a pose with her arms crossed over her chest. 'I believed that you saw it as your mission to tend our wounded men and ease their pain.' And as Charlotte smiled, she added, 'You've laughed twice in the last few minutes, Charlotte. That's more than I've seen you do in the last four months.' She linked her arm through

Charlotte's. 'If the thought of going to France can do that, then it has to be a good idea.'

Alex took a great deal of interest in Maggie's travel arrangements, asking her the name of the railway station from where she would be leaving and where she would arrive in London, the price of her ticket, and the places the train would stop on the way south. Normally she would have found him a dreadful nuisance, but they had become closer since John Malcolm's death, so she indulged him by telling him every detail and helping him look up street plans of Edinburgh and London. His teacher also encouraged his sudden interest in geography and lent him more books with maps of England and France and Belgium. Alex spent hours studying these, and when no-one was watching he copied the maps, and any useful information, into his notebook. By the time of Maggie and Charlotte's departure he had notes on every aspect of their journey.

Maggie's father accompanied both girls to Edinburgh to see them off. Maggie had waited until they had left the village before she told him that she might not return after her two months' training in London, but go instead to France. He became very silent throughout the rest of the journey, and it was not until they stepped onto the platform at Waverley Station that he spoke.

'I know that your mother will have talked to you about various matters as you became a woman, and also regarding the way of the world,' he began awkwardly.

'Yes, yes,' Maggie said hastily. She recalled her mother's embarrassed fumbling for words when some years ago she had tried to explain to Maggie the workings of basic bodily functions. 'I know all I need to know.'

'Few women have money, possessions or position in their own right,' her father persisted. 'But a woman does have the dignity which nature gave her, and she must use that to protect herself.'

'Nurses are given advice and strict instruction on their behaviour,' said Maggie, thinking to herself of how quickly she had ceased to be shocked by what she had seen and had to deal with in the hospital.

Her father was not to be deterred. 'You will be away from home. And if you do go to France you will meet men who have just been, or are about to go, into combat. You may feel very sorry for these soldiers and they may try to take advantage of you because of this.' He looked anxiously at Charlotte. 'Forgive me for speaking this way, Miss Armstrong-Barnes, but events have placed us in circumstances that we did not expect to find ourselves in, and your father is not here to advise you.'

'I do thank you for your concern, Mr Dundas,' said Charlotte, and impulsively she kissed Maggie's father on the cheek. He went bright red.

'No need for that,' he said stepping back quickly.

It was the first time Maggie had seen her father in such extreme discomfort. In the shop he was king in his own little kingdom; in the village which he rarely left he was a well-respected businessman.

As the train was about to depart Maggie also kissed her father. 'I hear what you are saying to me,' she said.

But later on the long train journey south she apologized to Charlotte for her father's behaviour.

Charlotte looked up in surprise. 'I didn't consider him to be at all rude. Any father or older brother would have done the same.'

'He is domineering,' said Maggie, 'and he wishes to keep myself and my mother contained in certain ways.'

Charlotte replied, 'Yes, but he does all this out of love for you. It was very difficult for him to speak out this morning. Yet he cares so much that nothing ill should happen to you that he takes the time to try to warn us both against the evils in the world.'

Maggie thought of her father's attitude towards her. 'Still, I feel that sometimes he is asking that I be less than I am.'

In London at the offices of the Red Cross the Sister gave Charlotte a searching look. She examined the certificates and letters of reference from the Cottage and the City Hospitals. She held out her hand. 'Birth certificate?'

Charlotte met her gaze with a cool smile and handed over her birth certificate with the altered date. The Sister's eyes narrowed and she glanced again at Charlotte. 'Do you have your parents' permission?' she demanded.

Charlotte kept her voice steady. 'My father is dead, my mother has written this letter.'

The Sister took a note of all Charlotte's details, kept the letter, and returned the certificates to Charlotte. 'You girls look younger by the hour.' She shook her head. 'Barely out of the nursery, and demanding the vote.' She handed Charlotte some papers. 'This is the information you need. Read it carefully. You can still withdraw at this stage. Please do not accept training unless you are absolutely serious about this. Contrary to any newspaper reports you will *not* be going on a picnic to France to meet handsome cavalry officers.'

From behind her in the queue Charlotte felt a nudge from Maggie, and she bent her head quickly to hide a smile as she replied, 'I didn't imagine it to be so.'

Chapter 24

CHARLOTTE AND MAGGIE spent most of December in London with friends of Charlotte's mother, and soon found themselves invited to various social events.

'My mother would be so happy to see me socializing in this way,' Charlotte confided in Maggie one evening as they returned from a dinner party. 'She didn't really approve of my taking up nursing but because of the War she could not object too much.'

'Don't you enjoy going out and about, not even a little bit?' asked Maggie, who found that she liked London a lot. Rather than being overwhelmed by the city as she thought she might be, she found it interesting to be in different company and have so many places to visit. Her expanding knowledge of art and literature heightened her appreciation of what she saw, and meant that she felt able to chat more confidently with Charlotte's friends and relatives.

‘I am impatient to be away.’ Charlotte spoke softly. ‘I feel that we are wasting time while men are dying in France and Flanders.’

At once Maggie felt embarrassed at sounding so trivial, and as if she understood the older girl’s feeling Charlotte covered Maggie’s hand with her own.

‘It’s just that for me London is so new and exciting—’ Maggie began to excuse herself.

‘I understand,’ Charlotte interrupted her, ‘and so it should be. It is only that I have been coming to the city every year since I was small, but this is your first time so it is right that you are so taken up with it all.’

The other person who knew how thrilling it must be for Maggie to be in London was Francis. At one time he had studied there and knew the galleries quite well. He sent her several hurried letters suggesting which ones to visit and what to see, and included some of his own personal notes on specific works. She wrote back quickly with her own comments and opinions. It seemed incongruous and certainly a little unfair that she should share famous works of art with him in this way. Outside Ypres his battalion occupied the trenches along the Yser Canal while across the Channel she stood, with his notes in her hand, gazing at a Botticelli *Madonna* or a da Vinci drawing.

When she mentioned this in a letter he wrote in reply:

My dear Maggie,

As I read your letters, in my mind's eye I see again these works of art, and I am able to enjoy them once more in a new way when you describe your own impressions of them. I would of course prefer to be in your company at this time. There is a great bond of feeling in mutual appreciation of any of the arts . . . music, literature and visual. However, even without war, people are constrained to be apart, but your letters I have with me always, and may read them at any time.

Francis

On Christmas Day Maggie and Charlotte declined invitations to go out. They had shopped the previous week and had sent Francis a box of presents. That night they sat by the fire and spoke little, but were each glad of the other for company.

After Christmas Maggie wrote to Francis to let him know that they would be moving on, and a few days later she received a letter that he had written to her during the last weeks of December.

Dear Maggie,

We have just come to the end of a most horrible period of time here, with an unusually high number of men being disciplined for offences. There had been one or two incidents in several of the Battalions – men lax on duty, slow to follow orders and suchlike. Some of them are half out of their wits with the noise or driven down by fear and cold, poor rations, and no hope of leave this winter. The last was hard for them to take with Christmas coming on, especially as the easing off from full hostilities due to the bad weather had made them hope that more would be able to go home and be with their loved ones at this special time of year. So morale was low, and the fact that we have gained little advances this year with a colossal casualty list had caused many to complain.

But some of the punishments seem barbaric – where a man is tied for hours to the wheel of a wagon, or deprived of food and kept in solitary confinement. It was all very unsettling, and week by week under shellfire Ypres itself loses definition. One can see clear across the town with few buildings left to block the view. To witness what was once such a beautiful place violated in this way is almost insupportable.

But the men are more cheerful now as Christmas was enjoyable. We commandeered a hop store and had full Christmas Dinner – we did not enquire too closely as to the origins of the meat – but it tasted good, washed down with beer and wine and followed by plum duff and rather a lot of rowdy songs – not quite what one was used to at home, but very heartening.

I thank you and Charlotte for the cake, the jam, the soap, the razor, the matches, the warm gloves, the new sketch-book and chalks, and all the many things you sent me. Most of all I thank you for your letters. I have no gifts for you but include some drawings to amuse you both.

The parcel included a bundle of sketches of soldiers at Christmas dinner, drawings of men eating and drinking.

Francis had also written to Charlotte and in the letter had said that he thought her too young to come to nurse in France.

Charlotte laughed as she showed Maggie this letter from Francis. 'He still treats me like a baby sister. He has even threatened to write and tell the authorities my true age.'

'Will he?' Maggie asked.

'Not at all,' said Charlotte. 'I think that he is coming to realize that I must make my own decisions about my life.'

Maggie admired Charlotte's courage at leaving the affluence of her home to volunteer near the Front, and she told her this.

Charlotte turned to her in real surprise. 'Oh, but you are so much braver than I, and have had much more to overcome to follow your own path. At one time I recall that the most serious decision I had to make was deciding which hat to wear. My mother and brother have always indulged me, whereas you have had to assert yourself in difficult circumstances.'

Maggie felt drawn to the younger girl by her appreciation, and realized that they both had overcome obstacles in lives which had originally been so very different.

'In any case,' said Charlotte, 'I think Francis is reassured because I will be with you, and I expect that we will receive special training before going abroad.'

'They won't send us out right away,' said Maggie. 'I am sure that we will be adequately prepared first.'

Maggie was right. In the New Year they were sent to train in the military hospital in Southampton, and it was not until Spring 1917 that they finally embarked for France.

1917

Chapter 25

'I ALWAYS HOPED THAT I should go to Europe,' said Charlotte, 'but I thought it would be a little grander than this.' The hospital ship was uncomfortably crowded with people and medical supplies, and the two girls were standing with a small group of nurses huddled at the rail as the ship sluggishly drew away from the dock before turning out into the Channel towards France.

Maggie, who had never even considered taking a European trip, smiled in reply. Despite the circumstances it was a thrill for her to be going on this journey, to a land where a foreign language was spoken and where she would meet people from many different places. The fact that this was only happening because her country was at war served to heighten the tension. Maggie thought of her twin brother. How excited John Malcolm and his friends must have felt as they set off on their great adventure as part of an advancing army.

The hospital at Rienne in northern France was more austere than either of the girls had expected. Although Charlotte having news from the two nurses from the Cottage Hospital who were stationed elsewhere in France, she was unprepared for the actuality of the working conditions. Marquee-style tents and long wooden huts were set around a large run-down chateau. This main building, which contained the surgical theatres and the nurses' quarters, was draughty and cold. Charlotte and Maggie were allocated a little cubicle to share. It contained two beds and a dressing table made from packing cases. At night from the east they could hear the sound of artillery fire.

Charlotte told Maggie about the young doctor in Springbank who had complained so loudly about the medical treatment of the soldier whose wound had turned gangrenous. 'It is amazing that the doctors and nurses here manage at all under these conditions,' she whispered to Maggie as they were shown round.

There was a steady flow of wounded, and their days consisted mainly of dressing wounds, and dealing with the tremendous number of men who had fallen ill due to the severe weather. The Army was feeling the effect of a most bitter winter, and the wards were full of cases of pneumonia, rheumatism and frostbite. What annoyed Maggie was her feeling that some of the conditions could be prevented, in particular those caused by the soldiers' own clothes. The puttees wrapped around the lower legs got soaked, dried, shrank, froze, and tightened like a tourniquet, cutting the blood supply to the feet.

'A simple change in the infantry uniform might help,' Maggie complained to Charlotte as they dealt with yet another case of frost-bitten toes.

But Charlotte adapted to the conditions much more quickly than Maggie. She is a nurse and I am not, thought Maggie. It is her vocation while I still am unsure as to where my life might lead. Maggie wondered if it was her new awareness and aspirations which made her discontented. She was now unable to accept things meekly. Perhaps her mother was right: one should keep to one's place in the world and be satisfied with that.

Another source of intense frustration to her was the disorganized method of obtaining any type of supplies. On the actual wards it was properly administered by the nursing staff, but to obtain anything involved pointless form-filling with frequently the wrong item arriving much too late.

One day in post-operative care Maggie was sent to the ward stores cupboard for one of the special citrate solution flasks needed to draw blood for transfusion.

The Ward Sister tutted impatiently as Maggie came back empty-handed. 'These items were requested days ago. There is a patient due out of theatre within the hour who must have a transfusion.'

Maggie volunteered to look in the supplies hut, and after searching there for many minutes at last found a box which contained the transfuso-vac flasks. The lid was off and the remaining vacuum-sealed flasks lying among the straw packing were cracked, rendering them useless. Maggie flung the box from her in a fit of temper. The flasks scattered and smashed on the floor. There was an exclamation from behind her. Maggie turned to find the Ward Sister standing in the doorway.

She was summoned to the Matron's office the next day.

'This is most serious,' the Matron began. 'Supplies are difficult to come by, and those in particular. We rely on public subscription and our accounts are inspected by appointed committees who award our allowances. To destroy precious equipment in bad temper is unforgivable.'

'The flasks were already broken,' said Maggie. 'And although I accept that I should not have lost my temper, I find it frustrating that our patients suffer needlessly because of inefficient administration, especially as it could so easily be better arranged.'

The Matron's face did not change expression. 'In what way?' she asked.

'The arrangement within the supply hut is very haphazard,' said Maggie. 'It is likely that the blood transfusion flasks were broken by someone looking for another item in a hurry. Also, the method of obtaining an item is time-consuming. Often the wards have to wait for essential supplies.'

'We cannot expect our supply base to anticipate our needs.'

'I think we can do that, to a certain extent,' said Maggie. 'My father did this in his shop and I helped him.'

'And?'

Maggie thought of her father's method of stock control in the shop at Stratharden, how he assessed his customers' needs and anticipated demand for special occasions such as Christmas. 'There are items that are required for almost every patient, and an adequate amount of these must be kept in stock all the time. But post-operative care is most crucial, and I think that we should look at how we can ensure that we never run short of surgical supplies.'

'It would be difficult to "pre-order" to any extent with accuracy,' objected the Matron.

'I don't agree,' said Maggie. 'It does need research and analysis, but information could be obtained from the medical officers, doctors, nurses, and even the patients themselves.'

'And the arrangement of the stores?'

Maggie thought for a bit. 'One would have to consult all the Ward Sisters and then devise a system which could cope with emergencies.'

'I see,' said the Matron slowly.

'It can be done,' said Maggie. 'And it would save time, effort and . . .'

'Prevent one from losing one's temper when one can't find something.' The Matron finished the sentence.

Maggie blushed.

Two days later in addition to nursing duties she was given supervision over supplies, to report directly to the Matron.

All her training in the shop, her stock management and book-keeping skills, were utilized. These, combined with her knowledge of the wards, helped Maggie overhaul the supply system. It was a task she enjoyed, finding it interesting and challenging, and she discovered that she had a flair for it. She could anticipate demand, and was better prepared than any other unit when an emergency arose. Soon the quarter-masters and warrant officers at the nearby army and air bases knew her by name and she made sure that she knew their names, and the names of all their children. Her fellow nurses were cajoled into knitting little mittens for any new baby expected by their wives. She made dressing dolls from the cardboard and paper packaging to send to their children at home. Thus her unit rarely ran short of any items. Often she took Charlotte with her on foraging expeditions, shamelessly using the young girl's soft beauty and vulnerable look to melt the hearts of crusty sergeants and wheedle equipment from the most reluctant army officer.

The Matron called for her when the reports had to be sent to the organizing committee and requests for more funds and equipment were submitted. When a group of hospital inspectors was due to visit, it was Maggie who organized their tour.

Rather than providing them with pages of dry information, Maggie had typed sheets with basic facts laid out: the number of wounded dealt with, number of operations performed; the turnover in laundry, linen, food and medical equipment, and how lack of the last of these could cost lives. She prepared a report on the new blood transfusion method introduced by the American doctors, with a note of the mortality rate before and after its use. Her report included a breakdown of costs, of the equipment needed, and the time required to train staff in its use. She told them the facts about gas gangrene and how it could be treated. Her best idea she held until the day of the inspectors' arrival, when she arranged to have Charlotte and another nurse change a particularly bad dressing during their ward tour. Using a hushed tone she issued the two women and two men with surgical masks.

'The smell will do you no harm,' she told them, 'but it can be overpowering. I would not wish you to experience any discomfort, although . . .' she paused, 'our nurses have to do this every day.'

Reckoning that their curiosity would overcome their aversion, Maggie was gratified to see them all slide their masks aside a little.

The Matron spoke to her afterwards. 'As a lesson in psychological manipulation it was a masterpiece.'

'Not too obvious, I hope,' said Maggie.

'It would not matter,' replied the Matron. 'The gravity of the subject presented in an intelligent way is what will impress them. It so often happens when women are involved in an activity that prejudice prevents us from being taken seriously.'

Maggie could not help but explore this small opportunity for intimacy. 'You mean that in a given circumstance women are not allowed to command the same attention as a man would.'

'I mean also that we can do ourselves a disservice by our behaviour.'

'We should be more vocal,' said Maggie.

The Matron smiled at Maggie. 'Ah, you are still young, Nurse Dundas. I myself have found that it is by deeds that we prove ourselves. I leave fine speechmaking to others. You must consider what you wish to do, and then act.'

Maggie saw that that was in fact what she herself had done, beginning by working in the munitions factory, and then by joining the hospital, and ultimately arriving here in France in her position of supplies administrator.

Chapter 26

MAGGIE HAD BEEN at the hospital for some weeks before her mail caught up with her. A small bundle of letters and drawings arrived from Francis, forwarded from her Southampton address. She read through them with increasing alarm.

My dear Maggie,

We came up from our rest billet the other night to relieve the troops in the front lines. I swear the times of our movements must be known to our enemies for they shelled the road as soon as we began, and stopped immediately we reached the communication trenches. We left the road at once and crawled through an orchard and some pigpens to reach our destination by another route. It seems incredible, but among this devastation the trees here are beginning to bud – after a bitter Winter, Spring now struggles to break through. As the thaw sets in it is the most punishing work to keep the trenches free of water. The pumps are poor excuses, and barely work. Our engineers have designed crude constructions which they call "duckboards" – long square poles of wood with thick crossbars set at intervals. These are made from whatever can be requisitioned, stolen or scavenged. Wood from shelled and bombed buildings, empty ration crates, wattle fencing, anything and everything is used.

My hotel view at the moment is out across the stretch of earth they call No Man's Land, and the very phrase sums up the waste of war – there is a solitary tree stripped of life and colour, spent ammunition, shrapnel and shells and . . . the unburied dead.

I am strangely unafraid of death; there is a trance-like quality to life under these circumstances. What frightens me more is the death of spirit, that I have so quickly become accustomed to the sights and sounds of war . . . such an ache in my head and in my heart.

Francis

The drawings with this letter were a mixture of pastel-shaded trees and hedges and several small detailed sketches of equipment and men sitting by the side of the road.

Dear Maggie,

Now it is the witching time of night, and I am with those on sentry duty in an advanced position. There are four other men with me and we take turns to watch in twos. To rest we slump against each other, back to back. In the main trenches the men can stretch out along the floor of the trench with the rats and the mud – perhaps not the best place to lie down. There are dug-outs to crouch in, and at places, boards have been set lengthways in spaces hollowed out of the trench wall. Some of these "bunk beds" are three tiers high, and are much sought after. At night sound travels. A struck match is like a pistol shot and occasionally I can hear the German soldiers talking to each other – not clearly as to distinguish their conversations, but enough to know it is a foreign tongue. Their language lacks the cadence of English and does not have the musicality of French, yet there is something attractive about it. The rough low tone has a mellow sound, and when it sometimes is accompanied by a quiet laugh then you know that a fellow soldier is sharing a joke with a comrade. It might seem odd to you that I write of our enemy like this, but it is a strange outlook that the British Tommy in the front line has for his deadly foe. When the shells are crashing round they curse them to hell and back, and if they appeared on the parapet then they would not hesitate to run a bayonet through them. Yet after an engagement I have seen one of our privates crawl out into No Man's Land, drag a wounded Hun over our trench top to safety and staunch the blood flow.

Suffering is the common lot of man.

As you might expect, men are jumpy in the dark and a sentry to our right fires a shot. Everyone leaps up and "stands to", but it is the movement of the moon behind a cloud. We can hear the poor chap being cursed, and we join in, although we know that we are just as likely to make the same mistake. And better mistaking shadows for an enemy and being alert, than thinking the enemy a shadow.

But shadows are in my mind.

Francis

Francis had included a black and white drawing of all that was left of the city of Ypres, showing the shattered Menin Road which led to the front lines. Francis had written below this scene of desolation:

The barbarians are triumphant. There is now little left of the beautiful Cloth Hall or the Cathedral.

There was no drawing or sketch with the last letter.

Dear Maggie,

The Captain with the pale eyes is no more. His head was taken off by a piece of shrapnel. I was standing not two feet from him when it happened. He was a cold unfeeling man, yet I find that I cannot rejoice at all in his death, as the same bombardment has taken away the men I had begged him in vain to supply with blankets. The stretcher-bearers are collecting remnants as I write this now . . . It is the death the infantryman fears most. They consider the bullet to be a much cleaner way to go. Myself, I would have the shell, if it came with a guarantee of absolute annihilation. I can think of no better way – sudden, swift, complete – to be obliterated, smashed to atoms. But then one would become an irretrievable part of this landscape, and I do not wish, in death, to be included in this desolation. What I long for most is that my bones rest somewhere where there is peace and light and trees and the song of birds, and children at play. This would seem a simple request, yet it has been denied to so many.

He had not signed this letter; it was as if he had broken off in mid-thought. Maggie put aside the long letter she had been writing to tell Francis all her news since she arrived at the hospital. Instead she wrote him a brief note and sent it at once.

Dear Francis,

I urge you to take some leave at once. Indeed, as your medical adviser I ORDER you to take leave. I send you my worst threat. I will not write again until I have heard that you have rested away from the Front.

If you cannot go to Britain, go to Paris, and do there whatever it is that young men do.

Chapter 27

I HAVE GONE TO THE WAR. I AM SORRY TO TAKE MONY FROM THE SHOP. I DID NOT HAVE ENUF IN MY TIN. I WILL PAY IT BACK. I WONT WRITE AS YOU MIGHT USE MY LETTERS TO FIND ME AND BRING ME HOME. ILL JOIN UP FAR AWAY AND NO-ONE WILL KNOW ME, AND I WILL GO TO FRANCE AND FIGHT. DONT WORRY.

LOVE TO MUM,
AND DAD

Alex didn't know whether to put a kiss or not. He knew that it was all right for soldiers to do that when writing to their sweethearts, but he couldn't remember whether John Malcolm had drawn a kiss in his letters to his parents. He couldn't go to the sideboard where his mother had put his brother's letters. She might see him looking at them, and then take more notice of what he was doing. Eventually he decided that a kiss to a mother was acceptable, but was still unsure about his father. He drew one kiss. If it was all right then his dad could share it.

Alex placed the letter in his school bag and set off in the direction of the village school. In the back lane he spoke to Hugh Kane.

'I feel sick.' He made retching noises.

'Want me to take you home?' Hugh asked him.

'Nah,' said Alex. 'I'll manage.'

Hugh didn't hesitate. There was always a game of football on the go in the yard before school began.

Alex waited, and then followed Hugh down to the end of the lane. He made a wide detour to arrive about five minutes later at the place where he had hidden his haversack, packed for his journey, in the field behind the school. The field where the soldiers had come and made camp on their recruiting march. The field where he had met his friend, Senior Private Cooper. Senior Private Cooper, whose name had appeared under *Died of wounds* in the casualty lists of yesterday's newspaper.

It was that which had finally made up Alex's mind it was time to go. That, and the announcement of the United States of America declaring war on Germany. Once the Americans arrived there would be no room for anyone else.

And it was now April. Alex knew the big battles usually began in late spring. If he didn't go now, it would be too late. It would all be over and there would be no Germans left. He would have no-one to kill to make up for the death of his brother, and his friend Private Cooper.

The head teacher came into the yard ringing the hand bell. Alex turned over onto his back and looked at the sky. Better wait a bit until the latecomers had gone past, and then he would creep into the yard and leave his school bag by the boys' toilets. It would be found later, but no-one would think much of it, until they realized he was missing and then the teacher, or his parents, would look inside and find his letter.

Alex watched the last trailing child go reluctantly inside. Now, he had one more thing to do before he could leave. Visit the house of his friend Hugh.

The back door was open as he knew it would be. Hugh's mother should have gone out by now. She earned a little money taking in washing, and she went off each morning with a big pram to collect it. It took Alex only a minute to find what he needed and then he slipped quietly out the way he had come in. He dodged over the coal-house wall and through the back lanes, expecting at any moment to hear an angry voice call after him, 'Stop, thief! Stop! Thief! Thief! Thief!'

He ran as hard as he could up the road to the farm. It was Wednesday and the lorry which collected the milk did the Edinburgh run today. His lungs were bursting and he had a stitch in his side as he arrived at the farmhouse. The dogs came rushing at him, barking, but he called their names and they stopped, recognizing him from his delivering his father's shop order. They licked his hand as he quietened them and Alex slipped round to the milking sheds. The lorry was still there! The driver stood by his cab chatting to the farmer and his wife. Alex crept forward quietly and scrambled up to find a hiding place, crouched down among the milk churns. A few minutes later the farmer came round and secured the tailgate. Alex heard the engine starting and the lorry bumped down the track to Edinburgh.

Alex left the lorry at its first delivery on the outskirts of the city. Although it meant more walking for him, he considered it too risky to wait on. He had all his maps with him and followed Maggie and Charlotte's bus route to Waverley Station. After buying his ticket he went to find his train. He made a point of asking the guard, the engine driver, and two different people on the platform if this was the London train. He decided not to take a seat. Better to keep moving about the train. That way no-one would be sure where he had actually got off. They were rattling across the long viaduct at Berwick before the guard inspected his ticket.

'Off to London, then, are we?'

'Yes,' Alex said loudly. 'I'm travelling all the way to London.'

The guard winked at him. 'Going to enlist, son? Better grow a moustache or you'll never get away with it.'

Alex smiled as he unwrapped his sandwiches. He had it all carefully planned. He *was* going to join up and he *was* going to get away with it.

Chapter 28

MAGGIE WAS STANDING by the open door of the supply hut supervising the unloading of a delivery, when a man in the uniform of an army lieutenant walked behind the lorry. 'Good morning,' he said, and touched the brim of his cap.

Maggie looked up, looked back at her supply checklist, and then dropped it and the box of bandages she had been holding.

'Francis!' she cried out. 'Oh, Francis.'

He took both her hands in his. 'God, you look wonderful,' he said. He stepped back and looked her up and down. 'A truly joyous thing to behold,' and he kissed her on the top of her head.

She thought he looked dreadful. Although he smiled at her, his face had lines she did not remember from when she had seen him last. His hands were restless, and he gripped them together tightly, clenching and unclenching his fists.

He noticed her anxious glances and smiled. 'I'm trying to break the nicotine habit, and it makes me nervy. When in the line, smoking is constant. It is the main way to relieve tension. The noise is relentless, unremitting. I have heard men weep to make it stop. And, of course, once you begin smoking you come to rely on it too heavily.'

Maggie said nothing, only slipped her arm through his as he talked, much as she had done those many months ago at the bus stop back home.

He gave a shuddering sigh. 'One's mind crawls with thoughts continuously. The only thing to do is to force another thought in, to push out the ones you cannot bear.' He stopped suddenly and turned to face her. 'I must tell you this, Maggie. Your letters are my lifeline. Your threat to stop them terrified me. Never stop writing to me, I implore you.'

He had twenty-four hours. Although Charlotte was unable to be free until the evening, Maggie did manage to change her shift, and as nurses and officers were not supposed to be seen off duty together, they borrowed bicycles and went out into the countryside for the afternoon.

Francis spoke about the coming Offensive. His battalion would be in a forward position just beyond Ypres, at a place called Langemarck, facing their objective of the Passchendaele ridge. He told her that one of his men, a platoon sergeant by the name of Seth Verrall, who had been in the push forward at Loos in 1915 and on the Somme in 1916, had begun to sob when he'd heard this news.

'He thinks that he'll never survive another battle, and the thing is, Maggie, he probably won't. The ones who lose heart completely seem to draw fire. The other men avoid them.'

The image of this man's face was in Francis's mind. Verrall had pulled off his helmet as he began to cry and Francis had seen the blue veins pulsating under the pale skin around the temples. The man's weeping had upset him deeply. He sympathized but was at the same time embarrassed by Verrall's breakdown in front of the others. Was it the man's crying that made him uncomfortable? Had Verrall started screaming or tearing off his uniform as some did, would he have borne it better? Did he despise the man because he had the courage to weep? He had little experience of this. A woman's tears moved him to pity. He had found it almost unbearable to watch Charlotte in the days following John Malcolm's death. One of the younger privates had grabbed Verrall's arm, and pleaded with him. 'Don't crack up now,

Sarge, or we're all done for.' The rest of the platoon had gathered round and eventually had coaxed and joked their sergeant back to a state of normality.

Maggie could only guess at the effect this scene had had on Francis. She watched his hands and his eyes, and guessed that one of his great fears was that he too would lose heart and infect his men. She tried to cheer him and told him stories from the hospital. His favourite was how both she and Charlotte had been glad to go to France to get away from the dreaded Sister Bateman, only to find on arrival that she too had enlisted and was in charge of their ward. For the first time in many weeks Francis laughed out loud.

They stopped at an estaminet and ate some bread and cheese. She noticed how the sunlight gave the soft yellow of his hair a golden depth. He caught her watching him and stretched his hand out and took hers. 'You are such a good sort, Maggie.'

It was the kind of thing her brother would have said. She was pleased, but at the same time strangely disappointed that Francis thought of her in terms of being a 'good sort'. Yet if she had been asked she would have been unsure as to what more she would have wanted him to say.

Later that night in the big recreation room, these thoughts were still in Maggie's mind as she looked at Charlotte. As soon as Charlotte entered the room she was surrounded by the men. Her fragile good looks seemed to make them want to protect her. Yet Maggie knew that underneath that gentle exterior was great strength. Charlotte was the one who could wash out the filthiest wound without flinching, and sat with death, stroking the hand of the failing young soldier, quietly talking down his terror. The screams and groans of the grievously wounded did not upset her. When Maggie had rushed to the rest room one day with her hands over her ears, Charlotte had come and put her own cool hand across Maggie's brow.

'How can you stand it?' Maggie asked.

'I think that any one of them might be John Malcolm and it makes it much easier.'

Now Maggie wound up the gramophone handle and put on a record. At once those who were able began to dance. Maggie stepped back and bumped into Francis.

'I leave in an hour, and came to spend some time with Charlotte, and say goodbye.' He glanced around. 'The Matron is not about, and I shall pretend that I am a patient.'

Maggie watched Francis as he danced with Charlotte. Their heads were close together as they talked and his arms encircled his sister as if to protect her. Maggie felt suddenly sad and did not know why. It is because he is going away tonight, she thought, and I will miss him.

Francis looked across Charlotte's shoulder and met Maggie's glance. In the space of a second Maggie's heart contracted and she caught her breath. When the record ended Francis came and stood in front of her.

'I really must leave now. Perhaps you would partner me in a waltz before I go?'

Maggie hesitated. 'I'm clumsy,' she said. 'You might be better with someone else.'

Francis smiled and took her arm.

They danced slowly without speaking. When it was over and they parted it seemed that something between them had changed.

Chapter 29

AS THE TRAIN left Newcastle Alex moved his position, walking down the corridor looking for anyone who might be getting off at the next stop. Eventually he found a woman with a baby and a young child who seemed to be collecting her things together. Alex stood close by her carriage door, and as the train slowed down and he saw the station sign for Durham his heartbeat began to quicken.

It was easier than he'd hoped. The woman gratefully accepted his offer to carry one of her bags and Alex took the hand of the child and helped him from the train. They moved together as a family group off the platform, and no-one gave them a second glance. Alex then went quickly to the gentlemen's toilet and changed into a pair of long trousers and some of John Malcolm's clothes that he had packed in the haversack. Now he was ready. He waited until another train came in before leaving the toilet and, mingling with the passengers, he walked casually to the exit. Ahead of him he could see the bulk of Durham Castle and the Cathedral Tower. He would get directions to the regimental headquarters from someone there.

The Recruiting Sergeant of the Durham Light Infantry put his chin in his hand and studied the boy carefully. He was quite a big lad, but a lad none the less, he was sure of it. Things had been tightened up after the outcry over fourteen- and fifteen-year-olds enlisting and no obvious under-agers had to be taken. But now they were so desperate for men that they could take them in at seventeen. And even if the parents found out later and objected, the boy couldn't be released as long as he had been passed medically fit as an eighteen-year-old.

'And you want to join the Bantams, you say?'

'Yes, please.' Alex stood as tall as he could and tried to deepen his voice.

'There was a whole Bantam Division, the Thirty-fifth, but it's been reorganized. There isn't a division specially for Bantams any more.'

Alex held his head up and tried to hide his disappointment.

'There's still our own Nineteenth Battalion.' The Sergeant spoke slowly. 'Although it's the Eleventh that's needing men at the moment.'

'Anything,' said Alex quickly. 'It doesn't matter to me which battalion I'm with.'

‘They’re Pioneers. That’s a lot of construction work, digging, laying telephone lines. Are you up to that?’

‘I am,’ said Alex confidently. He had after all dug a real trench with Sergeant Cooper.

The Sergeant looked at Alex. The boy was burning with it. Trying to act calm, and making a good job of it. But you could see that he was desperate to go for a soldier. It was a few years since the Sergeant seen that kind of enthusiasm, and it gladdened him to know that there were still some young men who wanted to fight back against tyranny. He guessed this one to be around sixteen, but he could be seventeen, in which case by the time his training was complete he would be old enough to serve. He was healthier than some of the older conscripts, and by his complexion, an outdoors boy. And he was fit. Not an underfed rickets-ridden slum dweller, glad to be given the chance of three square meals a day, but strongly built, country bred and fed. Could be an asset, and should be able to keep up in training and marching. He couldn’t place the strange strangulated vowel sounds. Scotch, he guessed, trying to sound English. Well, good for him.

‘Nice journey getting here?’ he asked in a friendly tone.

‘Yes, thank you,’ Alex said politely before he could stop himself.

'Aha, thought so!' said the Sergeant. 'You're from over the Border, aren't you?'

'Ah,' said Alex.

'I can always tell,' the Sergeant said. 'It takes a lot to fool me. What's your mother and father saying about all this?'

'They're dead,' said Alex. 'Da got killed in the Boer War.' Alex had heard Hugh Kane's stories a dozen times. He knew them off by heart, and repeated one of them now.

'And you think you could be a soldier, like your da?'

'Yes, sir!' said Alex. He saluted and stood to attention as Private Cooper had taught him.

The Sergeant nodded once or twice. 'You've got the look of a soldier's lad about you.' He hesitated. 'It would help if you'd a letter of some sort.'

Alex bit his lip to hide his smile of triumph. 'Will this do?' he asked. And taking Kenneth Kane's birth certificate from his pocket he laid it carefully down in front of the Sergeant.

Chapter 30

My dearest daughter,

Maggie, I am writing to tell you that Alex has gone to the War.

He left a note which says that there is no point in trying to get him back which makes me think that he had planned it out rather than just running away. He had become very secretive since you left. I knew that he had been taking things from the shop but had not said anything, thinking it to be boyish pranks and knowing how upset he was over his brother's death. I left him alone hoping he would come to himself in time. I know now that I should have seen his need and acknowledged it and spoken to him and I regret not doing this. He says that he will not write home as we may try to trace him by his letters, that he'll join a regiment far away from here so that he will be unknown to anyone.

Maggie, I don't know if there is anything at all that you can do. I went in desperation to Mrs Armstrong-Barnes who was very kind and helpful. She managed to find out through her contacts that a boy answering Alex's description was on the train from Edinburgh to London that day. We are quite definite about this as he spoke to several people and he told the guard that he was on his way to London. After that there is no sign of him anywhere. I have written to the War Office and they say that the recruiting officers look out for youngsters now and send them home as they have had so many complaints from mothers. I wonder how keenly they follow this, now that the War is in its fourth year and there is constant need for manpower.

Dear Maggie, your mother is quite ill with worry and I am very concerned for his safety.

Your loving father,
John Dundas

Maggie felt slightly sick. Alex had gone to enlist! She knew that there was tremendous pressure on the regiments to supply more men after the disastrous battles around the Somme. Alex was fairly tall and fit. He looked young, but they were so desperate for men now that they might not investigate this too deeply. At the earliest opportunity she showed her father's letter to Charlotte.

'You will write to Francis,' Charlotte suggested.

'Yes, of course.'

'I don't see what else we can do,' said Charlotte.

Maggie heard Charlotte say 'we' rather than 'you', and she wanted to hug her.

'He is a very clever boy,' said Maggie.

'If he is clever, then he will be resourceful,' Charlotte said.

'Yes, and we know how desperate they are for soldiers,' said Maggie.

The thought lay unspoken between them. They also knew what happened to these soldiers. Their wards were full of the maimed and sick.

Francis's reply, although immediate, was not encouraging. He concurred with both her and her father's fears that a keen recruiting sergeant would overlook Alex's youthful appearance.

If your brother says that he is seventeen, then he might be believed, and the Army can now take boys of seventeen years. Also, my information says that Parliament has allowed that a seventeen-year-old can be sent overseas to fight if he has the build and strength of an eighteen-year-old. I appreciate that this is not the news that you wish to hear but we have always been truthful with each other.

Alex's birth date was June 1901. Maggie calculated that her young brother was now almost sixteen, and a very healthy boy compared to some others, so the Army probably accepted him as being seventeen. Charlotte's birth date was January 1900 and she had passed for twenty. And Alex would most likely pass a medical as fit as an eighteen-year-old, and therefore might have been sent to France already. Maggie's spirits settled lower. Francis promised to search out whatever sources he could, and contact her again as soon as he had any information.

'The United States of America have joined the Allies,' said Charlotte. 'When their soldiers arrive, there will be less urgency to recruit in Britain.'

'Yes, but when will they arrive?' said Maggie. 'It takes time to train and equip men, and it is a long journey across the Atlantic.'

The Matron suggested that Maggie might wish to return home. 'Your parents now have no children at home. Perhaps you should consider where your duty lies?'

Maggie was suddenly conscious of the meaning of the Matron's words. She raised her head. It had not occurred to her to rush home to look after her parents. This in itself showed her how much she had changed.

'I would be very sorry to lose you, your organizational skills far exceed any army quartermaster that I've encountered. And your nursing is thorough. You are one of my most efficient members of staff.'

Under this wholly unaccustomed praise, Maggie's face went red.

When she left the Matron's office she went in search of Charlotte to ask her advice. Should she rush home? What good would it do? She recalled the day she heard of John Malcolm's death. It had been her mother who had been strong, when her father had ceased to function for several days. Did her mother abrogate responsibility because she had never been allowed to take it, other than for mundane tasks? Did this present generation of women, as the Matron had said, now use action to define themselves? The world would be a sorrier place without the actions of women. On a basic practical level, many men would have died. This was not because of them being women as such, but because of their skill, working as a fellow alongside men.

'We could go and stay in the Red Cross nurses' quarters in London for a few days,' said Charlotte slowly. 'My mother is living there now while our home is being used for convalescing soldiers. I could visit her while you make enquiries about Alex at the War Office. That might be more helpful than you going back to Stratharden. If you were making the enquiries in person then your parents would be more reassured. And both of us would benefit from a rest.'

Charlotte was right. Almost immediately on leaving France she and Maggie became young girls again. Although still obliged to wear their off-duty uniform they took advantage of the relaxation of discipline, and began to enjoy the absence of work and worry. London seemed a different city in warm weather, and the girls enjoyed the fresh air, free from the smell of blood and disinfectant. They walked in the parks admiring the flowerbeds of tulips and early roses, they ate in restaurants where there seemed to be very few restrictions on food, and often stopped to enjoy tea made from unchlorinated water.

The War Office was unyielding. Despite the letter that Francis had obtained for her from Major Grant they refused to let a member of the public have access to official records, especially in wartime. Through dogged persistence Maggie eventually wore down a clerk to give her some information on the recruits around the time that Alex had run away. She had a small moment of hope when he told her that the figure had been disappointingly low for the beginning of April. He came back after an hour or so. He was not allowed to give her the exact number but it ran to several thousands.

'Thousands!' she repeated.

He promised that he personally would search the lists name by name for that of her brother, and pay particular attention to the London regiments. When Maggie returned the next day she knew immediately by his demeanour that he had not found the name of Alexander Dundas. He was sympathetic but could do no more – although one comment he made lingered with her. Rather than try to find her brother only via the Army, perhaps she should think also of conducting her search from her brother's point of view. Was there any place or regiment that he had spoken about in particular? She resolved to write home and ask her parents to question Alex's friend Hugh Kane more carefully and to search thoroughly through any belongings Alex might have left behind.

In addition to making enquiries about Alex, Maggie took advantage of some free time to visit the bookshops. She had not imagined there to be so many books in the world, far less contained in one city.

'You should visit the British Museum, and the famous round reading room,' suggested one bookseller. 'It is a wonderful experience.'

Maggie spent a morning there while Charlotte visited her mother. Later that day in a small bookshop on Charing Cross Road Maggie fell into discussion with the owner about the purpose of literature, and its functions of shared observation and influence.

'Has there been anything written about the War?' Maggie asked him. 'Some article or commentary that is not official, not a newspaper report . . .' She struggled to explain what she meant. 'Perhaps something uncomplimentary, a piece of writing that would show what a person might truly *feel*. Rather than factual accounts, more the emotional impact. And also, perhaps, from the point of view of a person who might not wholly support the idea.'

'There have been poems, mainly in journals such as the *Westminster Magazine* or the *Cambridge Review*,' he told her, 'but there is a recent publication which might be of interest.' He brought her a slim volume bound in dark grey. '*The Old Huntsman* is a collection of poems by a young officer called Siegfried Sassoon. He has spoken out against the continuation of the conflict. His poems are sensitive and are becoming more well known.'

My dear Maggie,

This is the most precious, precious gift I have ever received. I carry it in my tunic pocket, which I am sure is against King's Regulations, but it means that I have it to hand. I am so glad that you said that you copied out your favourite pieces before sending it off to me, as I would hate to have deprived you in any way. Such comfort to know that I am not alone in my thoughts. If instead of speaking truth we remain silent, then surely our silence is a lie. To have this truth so eloquently scribed is a gift. A gift to have the poetic ability to write it, a gift to receive it, a gift to have a friend like you who would know that I wanted, indeed needed, such a gift, when I did not know it myself.

Yours ever,

Francis

Chapter 31

THE WORDS OF the poet resonated within Francis like a struck tuning fork. The desperate loneliness of his spirit was eased a little by Sassoon's poems of protest, anger and lament. In his billet at Poperinge as the weather became milder he managed to sleep better. He awoke in those first days of early summer to mornings mantled in blue and gold, and sought peace by drawing, reading and writing in the garden of the Talbot House all ranks club on Gasthuisstraat.

From there he wrote to Maggie, who had now returned with Charlotte to the hospital in Rienne.

Dear Maggie,

I admire the Belgians who have stayed behind, clinging to their piece of land and few possessions, living with the constant threat of shell-fire. There is a little girl here, Louise-Marie, whom the men have taken as a mascot. She lives in their stump of a house which stands like the last single rotted tooth left in an old head. Her mother keeps a cow and a few hens, which supply us with fresh milk and eggs, and the officers ensure that the cow is fed. Elsewhere, I've been told, a cow would disappear to end up in an army stewpot. The child runs about and the men have taught her some English. So many different regiments pass through that she has acquired a strange combination of accents. She can say "Aw Reet" for the Durham Light Infantry, and "I'm a bonnie lassie" to the Scots Guards. It cheers us all a great deal to see her tripping around the yard avoiding the dung heaps, and makes me think that perhaps it is all worthwhile. If in truth it is her that we are fighting for. Towards evening we often hear her mother singing softly a "berceuse" in their own dialect to hush the child to sleep.

The sun is shining, the air is soft with a pale promise of warmth to come. If the weather holds fine and we can move forward they might be able to rebuild their lives.

The next day the rain began.

Continuous, monotonous rain which ran off the roof of his billet, and quickly flooded the yard. Francis knew that nearer the Front the trenches and shell-holes would be filling with water. The frozen mud of the last winter had thawed to a gluey porridge and would now not have a chance to dry out. The constant shell-fire was systematically destroying the drainage system of the wet Flanders plain over which the infantry had to advance. Common sense dictated that they should cease the bombardment, at least until immediately prior to the order to attack, but field officer and private knew that this would not happen. The preparations had been made. The Offensive, although delayed, would take place. It had been planned, and like some unavoidable Biblical curse would continue. Inevitable, unchangeable, and doomed.

Francis went back up to the Front.

His men were digging assembly trenches, constructing dug-outs, laying cable. They worked knee-deep in slimy water, their feet dragging in a bottom coating of mud, the depth of which was rising daily. Day and night the air shook and the earth trembled with the sound of the guns. The utensils and equipment on the table and shelves in the dug-out rattled continuously. A deep raw pain settled behind Francis's eyes. He felt as though his brain was slowly detaching from inside his skull. The fine tenuous membranes which held it in place were tearing away one by one.

Dear Maggie,

A strange thing happened to me in the dug-out today. My whole being began shaking and trembling. At first I thought it was all within me, but then realized that I had no control over my limbs. I tried to grind my teeth and clasp my hands together but was unable. Nothing would stop it. The Captain gave me the brandy flask and ordered me to drink as much as I could get down in one gulp. I did, though he had to hold the flask to my mouth and I tried to force the neck between my teeth but they were chattering so much that it slopped over my tunic, and what did go down gagged in my gullet and drove tears into my eyes. And then suddenly I realized I was crying, whether from fear or shame I do not know. My face was running with tears. But this officer stood talking quietly to me and blocking any view others might have of me until the moment passed. With great effort I managed to pull myself together and I stammered an apology. I could not look him in the eye. He gripped my shoulder and said, "First days back in the front line, under heavy shelling – it'd be bloody strange if you didn't have a reaction."

Later the Battalion Major came down to my dug-out and invited me for a walk along the trench so I knew something was up. He suggested I might spend some time attached to Brigade H2. When I say "suggested" it is more of a command. He made some pretext by saying that he had noticed my sketches and thinks that I would be useful in reconnaissance and mapping. I protested. I feel it to be such an unworthy thing to do, to leave the men. He would not be moved. He has judged me to be "windy", and wants me away so that I may have no adverse influence. I keep thinking if it had been some other poor sod he might have been shot for cowardice in the face of enemy fire. I am to go to Farnborough in England to undergo training in recognition and analysis of aerial photographs, and attend a map-making course. This is a great setback for me. In all the trials my nature has had to accommodate in my experience of war this is the most difficult to bear. To become a "staff" so despised by the men, one of the red tabs who rarely venture forward to see what conditions those they command have to suffer. I must comply, but have requested that it be a temporary secondment.

As the staff car carrying Francis made its way towards Brigade Headquarters, the 11th Battalion of the Durham Light Infantry marched to their billets in a barn in the Ypres Salient. The Private known as Kenneth Kane crept into a corner, utterly exhausted.

'Sleeping like a babe,' said the Sergeant.

'That's because he *is* a babby,' said his Corporal, Eric Kidd.

'He's supposed to be with the Nineteenth. He's a Bantam, that's why he's small. His papers say he's the right age.'

'Dinna care what his papers say. Just need tae look at him.' Eric Kidd went over to the young boy he had befriended. Pulling some straw from a bale, he threw it over Alex. 'Criminal, that's what it is.' He went to the door of the barn and stood with the Sergeant looking out at the heavy skies emptying rain. 'Weather just like home.'

The Sergeant looked at the sky and then at the land. 'Yes, but at home we've got the hills for it to run off, and the sea for it to run into. Here they've to break their backs digging ditches to gain a field of usable farm soil. If this doesn't get drained off as it's coming down, by a week or two we'll be fighting in a swamp.'

Chapter 32

RETURNING FROM HIS training in England, Francis made a detour to see Maggie and Charlotte.

He took them both to tea in Le Touquet, where they ate cake which Francis had brought from England and drank the local delicacy of *chocolat chaud* served in wide earthenware bowls. After an hour or so, Charlotte declared herself tired out and opted to return to Rienne, while Francis and Maggie went for a stroll in a little copse which overlooked the beaches. The woods were full of early bluebells, so thickly clustered under the trees that their definition blurred to a haze of azure. It reminded both of them of home.

'If it weren't for the sound of the guns we might be in Stratharden,' said Francis.

'When this is over,' said Maggie, 'I hope never to hear the sound of guns again. The Matron says that gas gangrene and septicaemia claim more lives than direct gunfire. War has become an industry, and yet the medical advances are enormous. We can transfuse blood, halt infections and sometimes save those with sepsis. Should we be glad that a positive good has come out of it all?'

'I think that increasingly war will be industrialized,' said Francis. 'Who knows, it might even become helpful to the economy. But let's not talk of war. It's almost too real to be discussed.' He put his head on one side. 'You have cut your hair.' He studied the brown hair curling softly from under her nurse's cap. 'Yes,' he said finally, 'I think it suits you, very up to date and in the mode.'

'It was not a decision made with fashion in mind,' said Maggie. 'Short hair is much easier to keep clean. You soldiers are very generous with your presents, and bring lice on every visit you make to the hospital. They are resistant to anything and everything we try to use to overcome them.'

Francis said teasingly, 'I thought nursing was a genteel business. The journals and newspapers show wonderful images of our nurses looking very fine in starched whites; decorous ladies quietly tending to our stricken soldiers.'

Maggie laughed as she thought of the rush in the wards when ambulances full of wounded men arrived. 'My mother says that you can always tell a lady by her hands.' She held her own hands out in front of her. 'I am a lost cause.' Her hands were red and chapped with many little cuts and sores.

'To avoid infection we swab our hands with disinfectant rather than cold cream. It doesn't enhance their appearance at all,' Maggie said ruefully.

Francis stopped, took her hands in his and turned them face upwards. 'They are the loveliest hands I have ever seen,' he said.

Maggie was aware of her heart thudding, slow, deliberate and heavy in her breast. She took a step back and looked up at him. He is my friend, she told herself, nothing more.

Francis lifted her right hand and placed it along his cheek. Her fingers stretched almost to his ear, her palm cupped his chin.

His face was gentle, pliant to the light pressure of her touch. Maggie had always supposed that a man's face would be rough with constant shaving, but the skin under her hand was as soft as chenille.

Francis laid his own hand over hers and slid his fingers out to cover each of hers. He closed his eyes, his lips barely parted as he whispered, 'I want to remember your touch.'

For a moment Maggie held the warmth of his face in her hand; his breath fluttered at her wrist. Neither of them spoke. Then he opened his eyes and smiled.

'We had better return,' he said.

She didn't reply. Was this falling in love? Why didn't she know? With Charlotte and John Malcolm it was plain to them and everyone else. They were flying, able to see stars, high, bright and clear in the sky. Why had she, Maggie, then this upside-down sensation? The more she thought to try and analyse the situation, the more confused she became. Should she not think about it, just seize the moment? But that was not her way. Nor his.

'Yes,' she replied finally. 'We had better return.'

The one thing she did know, whether this was love or not, was that she had the best friend that it was possible for her to have. She had bonded with a person who sought to understand her. Francis had made her see that horizons were for going beyond. She had learned from him, and unbelievably, he from her. It was not one feeling but many, sensations which she found intellectually and physically moving. All this was humbling yet, in a quiet way, exciting.

On her return to the hospital at Rienne, the moment on the path in the woods with the bluebells at her feet stayed with Maggie. And helped sustain her through a long and difficult week when she and Charlotte sat with one of their youngest patients, a boy of eighteen, aware that he was slipping away from them. Towards the end he spoke some words, and died. Both Charlotte and Maggie were badly affected, and readily took the offer from the other members of staff who volunteered to lay out the body if they would sort through his things.

In the breast pocket of his tunic there were some muddied pieces of paper. Maggie was about to discard the sodden bundle when Charlotte took it from her hand.

Charlotte carefully unfolded the crumpled packet. She separated the pieces and laid the letters out, one by one, along the window ledge.

'They'll dry off there,' she said.

Maggie shook her head. 'He must have carried them with him when he went over the top,' she said. 'He had lost his boots but not these.'

'I think all soldiers appreciate any form of contact with the rest of the world,' said Charlotte.

'These letters in particular must have meant a great deal to him.'

Charlotte looked across at Maggie. 'My brother appreciates your letters in particular. He tells me that you preserve his very sanity.'

Francis knew that he was losing his mind. It would not happen in any acute dramatic way, as when once he had seen a man throw down his weapon and begin a hysterical, screaming, babbling rant. For himself, he had embarked on a slow terrifying journey into madness. As the mud from Salient to Somme swallowed tanks, men and horses, Francis felt it suck at his mind, pulling him down inexorably. He travelled up and down the road between Brigade and Divisional Headquarters, briefing and debriefing the pilots on the reconnaissance flights, interpreting the photographs and compiling his maps of death. Conversations and meals with others were required routines which he performed with his body while his mind functioned elsewhere. At night when he lay in bed he could neither recall whom he'd spoken to, nor what food he had eaten that day. He knew that the photographs of the devastation which he studied were accurate recordings of what was happening on the ground, not an imagined scene or an artistic interpretation. Rather than being pleased that his particular skill for drawing was being utilized, Francis saw his work as some hellish punishment for his talent.

He imagined how it must be for the troops trying to advance in these conditions. The infantry struggling to breathe in a gas attack, blinded, and in terror of leaving the safe path. He dreamed of the mud, and all life suffocating in it. Images moved in front of his face as he lay on his canvas trestle bed. He stared at the night sky through his uncurtained window and the pale drum-skin of the moon beat inside his head.

And then the child Louise-Marie was killed. A shell landed in the yard of their little dwelling and buried her and her mother alive. Soldiers dug with their bare hands to reach them. It was a day when he was in Poperinge and had gone to see his friends in his old billet. Francis arrived at the house as they were bringing the bodies out. Their cow had somehow survived. The sight of the beast dragging grass from the remainder of the wall enraged Francis and he wanted to kick it. Soldiers who had seen every type of horror over the last three years stood about, useless and grief-stricken.

'For God's sake, get rid of that animal!' he heard himself yelling, and then he turned away and vomited in the road.

The incident acted as a catalyst for Francis. Men were dying in their hundreds daily. High Command would not let up on the Offensive. The infantry must struggle on and gain what ground they could before another winter set in. Francis resolved that he would ask to be allowed to return to a forward position. But first he would go and see Maggie.

Chapter 33

MAGGIE AND CHARLOTTE both went to the funeral of the eighteen-year-old boy they had nursed. A roughly made wooden cross with his name and age inked on it, *Richard Chalthorpe, Age 18,* was placed over his grave. Charlotte and Maggie waited behind after the grave-diggers had gone and laid some small stones around the edges to mark his place. Charlotte had pulled some violets by the roots and scraped a small hole with her fingers in which to place them.

Later that afternoon Charlotte and Maggie were sorting laundry when they were called to the Matron's office. An elderly couple were sitting there. The Matron introduced them as the parents of the boy who had died.

'Mr and Mrs Chalthorpe, these nurses tended your son, and were in fact with him when he passed away.'

The boy's mother spoke slowly. 'He was our only son, our only child in fact. He was born when we had given up hope of ever having any.' She looked at Charlotte and Maggie, a bewildered look on her face. 'We got word that he was very badly wounded, not expected to live, but we thought if he saw us it would help. We came as quickly as we could . . .'

'We booked a passage right away,' said the man. 'But we arrived too late. We are here now, and he is dead and buried.'

'I knew that he was very ill,' said the woman, 'but I hoped . . .'

Charlotte crossed the room and knelt down in front of the boy's mother. She took the old woman's hand in her own. 'Even if you had been here it would not have saved him. His time had come and he was very content as he passed away. He believed that his life had been fulfilled and that he was going to God. He was glad that he had not let anyone down, that he had done his duty.'

'That is what he said at the end,' added Maggie. The boy's father looked at her. His eyes searched her face, desperate for any information she could give him. Maggie nodded. 'Your son said, "I did my duty." He was so proud of himself.'

'As you should be too,' said the Matron briskly, but not unkindly. She motioned for Charlotte to rise. 'I will take Mr and Mrs Chalthorpe to visit the grave. I would like you both to gather up their son's personal possessions and bring them here to my office where they can collect them before they leave to go back to England.'

Maggie and Charlotte went through the dead soldier's haversack, separated out the army issue items, and collected together the boy's personal possessions. It made a sad little bundle: his letters and some picture postcards, a hand-knitted balaclava, a pair of monogrammed nail scissors, a little leather pocket book and several family photographs. There was a tobacco tin with the words 'To Richard, much love, Mother & Father'.

Charlotte and Maggie delivered the package to the Matron's office and went to take some tea in the rest room.

'That was such a heartbreaking thing to do,' said Maggie.

'Yes,' said Charlotte, 'but his parents will be so glad of it. When they come to look at all his things, it will give them time to think about him, and hopefully bring comfort . . .' Her voice tailed off.

'Unlike us.' Maggie voiced their unspoken thoughts. 'We have none of John Malcolm's belongings returned to us, no grave to grieve over.'

'I have very little to remember him by,' said Charlotte. 'His letters and a daisy chain.'

'A daisy chain?'

Charlotte smiled. 'You probably don't remember that day in August. It is almost two years ago now, when Francis drove us all in the car to picnic. Your brother made me a daisy chain, and we laughed because he was so clumsy and couldn't thread the stems properly.'

A sudden memory came to Maggie of that outing and of her jealousy as she watched Charlotte and her brother, close and laughing together. It seemed now to Maggie such an unworthy sentiment to be provoked by this girl who appeared to have no rancour against the world that had robbed her of her love. No bitterness nor resentment poisoned her mind. She directed all the love she had into looking after the wounded and dying. Her sympathy in going forward to take the hand of the mother of the dead boy earlier was so genuine, Maggie knew that although the Matron had not approved, she would find it difficult to reprimand Charlotte for showing such unaffected compassion. Her gentleness and sweetness were known throughout the hospital and village. The French staff and patients called her *La Petite Sourire* because she always smiled, no matter how grim the task she was performing.

Maggie left Charlotte to make the tea and went to her room. She searched in her suitcase until she found what she was looking for, then she returned to the nurses' parlour.

'I have something to show you.' Maggie handed a picture of her brother to Charlotte. 'It is a photograph of John Malcolm. I'm afraid I can't remember exactly when it was taken.'

Maggie heard Charlotte's sharp intake of breath. The young girl held the photograph in one hand and with the fingers of the other touched the face of the boy laughing out at her.

'I think it may have been taken about two years ago,' said Maggie, 'so he looks a bit younger. In fact he would be about the age you are now.'

'Oh.' Charlotte bit her lip and her fingers clenched together.

Her face had such a piteous expression, that Maggie impulsively said, 'You may have it, if you wish.' And as Charlotte's wide grey eyes looked at her disbelievingly, Maggie repeated, 'Please keep it. He . . . I want you to have it.'

Charlotte's eyes filled with tears. 'Thank you,' she whispered, 'thank you.' She swallowed, and as she did she felt the lump that occupied the cavity of her chest move a little. She had lived with it for so long that she had become used to its presence within her. But now it seemed as though the ragged edges which sometimes threatened to tear her apart when she breathed had dulled just a little. She stepped forward and kissed Maggie on the cheek, then hurried from the room.

Maggie put her hand to her face where Charlotte had kissed her. It was such a *sisterly* thing to do, and Maggie, who had never had a sister, was overcome by the gesture.

Maggie went back to her duties. Usually she regretted things done on impulse. In the past her quick temper often left her with an unpleasant aftermath of her words or actions. That afternoon as she worked she waited for the let-down feeling that would come with the realization that she had given away her precious photograph. It didn't happen. She knew by Charlotte's reaction that it had been the right thing to do, and within herself she felt only peace.

Chapter 34

IT WAS DIFFICULT for Maggie to concentrate on her work when her mind was constantly filled with thoughts of Alex. She, like her father, had feelings of guilt about the time she had spent with her younger brother. Perhaps if she had paid more attention she would have noticed what he was about. Why had she not thought his deep interest in her travel arrangements unusual? The words of the clerk in the War Office in London came back to her, and she tried to think of how Alex might plan his running away. Her father had written to her again saying that he was absolutely sure that Alex had gone to London because he himself had gone into Edinburgh and spoken to the guard on the train that Alex had travelled on. The man remembered inspecting the ticket as the train went through Berwick, and the boy saying quite specifically that he was going to London. Maggie pondered on this. It seemed strange that Alex, who had taken such care that no-one saw him leaving the village, should draw attention to himself in this way. Unless … Maggie gave a little cry aloud. Of course! Alex was clever and resourceful, as Charlotte said. They should not be contacting every London regiment asking for information, they should be trying anywhere *but* London. And then Maggie remembered the maps that she had shown Alex, and his interest in all the different regiments. It was so obvious! Somewhere on the journey south he had got off the train, after leaving them a false trail to follow.

Maggie was annoyed at herself. To be fooled so easily and for so long had probably lost them any chance of finding him. Because of her lack of thought Alex might be dead, or lying somewhere in a hospital not unlike this, his face wearing that half-crazed battle-weary appearance.

Many of the wounded Maggie nursed had that look. She had come to an understanding that it was more than just the pain they suffered. These men had images and memories in their heads that they couldn't dislodge. She would reason to herself that if she could pull their minds away for even a short time then it should be beneficial. So she tried to supplant their dark thoughts with some other. She would chat and tell them about herself and her home, describing her father's shop, the village and the hills beyond.

She was attending to a wounded man, Robert Ashley, a captain in the Essex Regiment, and mentioned her father's name being over the shop door, when he suddenly said, 'Dundas? You said Dundas?'

Maggie nodded.

'I met a soldier called Dundas. He was with the King's Own Scottish Borderers . . . in July 1916 it was . . . he died beside me in a shell-hole on the first assault on the Beaumont Hamel ridge.'

Maggie's hand ceased tucking in the sheet. She stood completely still without straightening up. 'My brother was killed at the Somme in July 1916,' she whispered. 'He was in the King's Own Scottish Borderers.'

Robert Ashley put his hand over hers where it rested on the bedcover.

'I am very sorry,' he said.

'What was it like?' she asked him. 'Was it awful?'

He looked away from her down the ward, as if not seeing the rows of beds with the injured men and the orderlies moving around.

'I don't remember,' he said.

And she knew that he lied. That there was a great and terrible deception being acted out . . . Maggie shook her head. She would not be part of it.

Their eyes met. 'Tell me,' she said.

'It was a living hell,' he answered her quietly. 'Unbelievably so. We might as well have sent a visiting card to let them know the exact time of our arrival. The wire on our side was ordered to be cut days before the attack to give a way through, and some of these paths were marked out with coloured ribbon for us to follow. Boards were laid down over the front trenches so that the men at the back could rush forward. The Germans couldn't help but notice it. And they must have seen all the build-up of supplies and troops in advance. Our heavy bombardment didn't crush the enemy; they were dug in too deep, and when it stopped, they knew we were about to attack. As we came across they were waiting for us. Their machine-gun fire brought us down in lines as we advanced.' He passed his hand over his face. 'The Inniskilling Fusiliers were first over the top, and your brother's battalion followed them in. A flare went up from the other side to launch their counter barrage, and in the confusion it was read as a signal from our troops that some of them had taken a position. We were sent in at about nine o'clock in the morning and had to climb over these two battalions, dead and dying, to try to get through. When the remains of the Essex got to their wire it had hardly been damaged by our guns, and that's where the rest fell.'

Maggie felt as though she had been struck across her heart. 'Oh God,' she said. 'Oh God.'

Robert Ashley went on slowly. 'I took two bullets in the leg and crawled into a shell-hole. Your brother was there. He was smiling. He thought we were winning and he was proud that he had done his bit. I didn't tell him otherwise. I gave him some water and talked to him, but he was dying. I'm so sorry,' he said helplessly. 'There was nothing more I could do. A medic had been to him, and given him morphine, so he wasn't in pain. He slipped away quietly.' Robert looked at Maggie directly. 'Truly he did. I promise you. Like a baby falling asleep.'

Maggie's eyes and heart were full. She was glad to know that her brother had been resolute and brave. To know that he had died thus, and not choking on the dreaded poison gas, or withering with a gangrenous wound. That he had had such a companion by his side made it so much easier to bear.

'This is tough for you,' said Robert Ashley.

Maggie smiled at him. 'It's . . . it's so good to hear that he had someone with him when he died. He was fortunate that it was you.'

'I wish I could tell you more,' he went on. 'Oh, there was one thing. Near the end, he mentioned someone's name. I thought it must be a fellow soldier or a mate of his from home. Just before he slipped away, he said "Charlie" soft like, as if it was someone special.'

Maggie waited a full hour for Charlotte to come off duty. She watched her approach before Charlotte saw her. It struck her how contained Charlotte was, how much her demeanour had changed since the earlier times when she had known her. Maggie remembered the day on the bridge when she had gone to tell Charlotte of John Malcolm's death. How thin Charlotte's bones had seemed as she had held the taller girl in her arms. And how, since then, her youthful energy had been replaced with a more subdued manner.

Charlotte straightened a little when she saw Maggie and said a cheeful 'hello'.

What a torture it must be for her, thought Maggie, who lived with her own pain each day. How strong she was to bear it without complaining. She gripped Charlotte's arm. 'Come with me,' she said. 'There is someone you must meet.'

By good fortune Robert Ashley was sitting alone by his bed when they arrived. Maggie sat Charlotte down in a chair beside him. 'Captain Ashley, this lady was a very good friend of my brother's. I know that she would very much like to hear about his last moments with you in the shell-hole. Will you tell her exactly what you told me?'

Then Maggie left, closing the door quietly behind her.

Chapter 35

IT WAS ALMOST eleven o'clock in the evening when Maggie, walking with another nurse, Mary Gardner, towards their quarters in the château, saw the soldier standing underneath one of the plane trees which lined the driveway. As they passed he spoke her name softly.

'Maggie?'

'Francis!' Maggie's delight, instant and uncontrived, caused Francis to tremble in relief and joy.

'I've only got a few hours . . . can you spare any time?'

Maggie spoke to Mary Gardner. 'I won't be too late,' she said.

Mary Gardner laughed. 'Be as late as you like, love,' she said. 'I'll leave the lavatory window open and put a pillow in your bed just in case.'

'I only called in to say hello,' said Francis. 'There is an attack planned. We are making the final assault.' He grimaced. 'I suppose, more accurately, I called in to say goodbye.'

Maggie put her hand to her mouth. It was his demeanour more than the finality of his words which alarmed her. His eyes were hollow, as though he had blanked out feeling and thought and was now living with nothingness. She was terribly afraid.

'Don't look so worried, Maggie—' Francis broke off as he began to shake, his whole body surrendering to violent spasms, head rolling and limbs jerking.

Maggie grabbed his hand. 'Let's find somewhere.' She glanced around, and realizing that she carried the key to the supplies hut, half supported him there. 'Here, sit down.' By the moonlight through the window she rummaged among a bundle of blankets and made a space for both of them to sit on the floor.

'I'm so sorry,' he said more calmly.

'You should not apologize for being afraid of death,' said Maggie.

'It is not my own death that holds me in terror. That would be such a release. It is all the others.'

Maggie recognized his deep trauma. She had seen it before, but in all the rush on the wards the nurses had little time to spend to ease the minds of the wounded men. It was the physical side they concentrated on. They had to. Men would die if they didn't. But you did your best to lift their spirits, patting hands and joking with them. And there were the ones whom you went back to and sat with during your free time, to help them through their rough patches. The more serious cases they never saw. Men diagnosed with nervous debility were removed as quickly as possible. Maggie knew at the beginning of the War some had been shot for cowardice, and even now if they could be patched up and sent back they were.

Maggie did not wish to reduce Francis in any way by her behaviour, but talking through this seriously with him seemed an inadequate response.

He was still shaking badly as they sat down, and his voice when he tried to speak came in ragged gasps of broken sound.

Maggie remembered her parents' reaction to the telegram telling them of John Malcolm's death. Her father scraping his chair back from the table, and then folding in upon himself, unable to get up. Her mother rising quickly to go to him. Standing beside his chair, she took his head in her hands and turned his face towards her womb to press him close. He had put his arms around her waist, and she had rocked him, patting his head over and over, saying, 'Hush, hush, now. Hush, hush.'

Maggie turned to the trembling man by her side, reached out her arms and pulled him against her. 'There now,' she said quietly. She slid further down with him among the blankets so that they were lying side by side. 'Lie quiet here for a bit,' she murmured, and she cuddled him against her own body.

After a while the racking sobs stopped and the juddering in his limbs quieted. As she held Francis close and comforted him, Maggie felt something stir physically within her. She drew back a little to look at his face and see if he could be somehow aware of this without her having spoken.

He was asleep. His breathing shallow but steady, his eyelids still.

Finally Maggie slept too, lying on the rim of consciousness, listening like a mother for a sick child in the night. But when, near to morning, she awoke and looked into his sleeping face her own breath quickened again and she ached to kiss him. She contented herself by stroking his cheek gently to awake him.

Francis, wakening, saw Maggie's face and thought he was dreaming. Even as he reached out in his dream and touched her cheek, he was only obliquely aware of how vivid this dream had become, and it was not until she spoke that he realized she was real. And then he wept for it being real, as had he been dreaming he could have prolonged this wished-for state, but now in reality he would have to say farewell and leave her.

Maggie seeing this, and thinking it to be his terror at returning to the Front, thought her heart would break. Her mind desperately seeking a solution she whispered, 'I could speak to one of the doctors. He would prescribe complete rest. You would be excused duty and—'

Francis gave a shuddering sigh and put his finger to her lips. 'No, no. I am not afraid to go back. It is the pity of it all that overwhelms me from time to time. And seeing your beautiful face beside me as I awoke serves to underscore all the horror.'

Maggie felt her throat contract. No-one had ever before said that she was beautiful. When she was small her father had called her his 'bonnie lass', but 'bonnie' was not 'beautiful', with all its overtones of sophistication, power and permanence. Now, as previously her mind had been drawn to this man, she felt her body warming, and she leaned to him.

Francis sighed again. He put his hands on her shoulders and made a little space between them. 'We must be sensible,' he said softly.

'I don't feel very sensible at the moment,' Maggie whispered and put her head against his neck.

'I know,' said Francis, 'I know,' and he stroked her hair for many minutes until there was no more time left for either of them.

Chapter 36

AS FRANCIS RETURNED to the Salient, the depleted 11th Battalion of the Durham Light Infantry was regrouped to the 19th Battalion. Alex, Corporal Eric Kidd and those soldiers of the 11th that remained from the struggle around the Menin Road were to have respite leave in Poperinge before travelling by train, bus and lorry to the Somme.

Alex knew that the main reason he had survived the battle zone around Ypres was Corporal Eric Kidd. The older man had minded him ever since they had arrived at the Front. And Alex also knew that it was more than just his life that Eric was concerned about. The Corporal was troubled by Alex's reasons for joining up.

'Revenge sorts nothing, son,' he said, when Alex eventually told him why he had enlisted. 'Your brother is dead. If you kill all the Germans in the world, he'll still be dead. Get revenge out of your head, and make room for your heart to grieve.'

On the journey down to the southern part of the line the men talked of their part in the ongoing action in what the officers were calling the third battle of Ypres. Alex had always imagined that being in a battle would be a definite thing. Commanders would lead at the front, and everyone would know exactly what was happening. He had thought almost that he would be able to watch the action as well as take part. He had not envisaged the mess, the chaos, the running and shouting, the unbearable noise, and the overwhelming awfulness of it. He had been part of the great push that was still going on, and had no clear awareness of what was actually happening. It was his first experience of an attack and he had hated everything about it. There was no excitement, no joy of marching forward together to defeat the enemy, only a dull tense pain of dreadful anticipation in his gut and then an explosion of gunfire and confusion. On his first engagement a man had fallen and died right in front of him, and when Alex had stopped and bent over to see if he needed help, Eric had grabbed him by the collar and dragged him away.

'Stretcher-bearers will get him, son.'

'No they won't,' said Alex. The truth of what he had said sinking into his consciousness as he spoke. Throughout the fighting the bodies just lay there and eventually decomposed or disappeared into the mud.

There were newspaper reports which the men talked about. People were saying that 'their boys' were beginning to win through. Alex had no idea of what ground they had gained. If anybody had asked him where he had fought, he would not have known.

Francis did know. Through his reconnaissance work he was aware of every intimate atom of earth which made up the sodden torn-up ground. He pored over the aerial photographs studying the nuances of shape, size, shadow and tone. And what he did not know, he imagined.

He wrote to Maggie:

To say that mud surrounds us is inadequate. We are in the belly of the beast. They are trying out tanks. It is outrageous. Men and horses are sinking; how can anything heavier survive? The enemy have the mark of our few passable tracks, and yet still we are to push on. Wattles and willow hurdles are gathered and all flung down to try to stop men sinking in the evil treacherous filth.

I am shaking as I write this, having just been part of an incident with one of the limber teams. A horse had missed its footing and been caught in a mud-filled shell-hole. Its eyes rolled crazily in its head as it struggled to free itself in vain. The more it flailed about, the more it hastened its sinking further. The men watched helplessly and I could bear it no longer. I got a rope round my waist and leaned out as far as I dared and shot the poor beast between the eyes. I think it knew, because as it watched me as I came close, it became still, accepting its fate.

I think I am now ready to accept my fate, which may be that I am not to die, but to live with this for the rest of my life. We cannot come out of this as the person we were when we entered. No-one can.

Francis's insistence on being given an active role eventually led to him being attached as an intelligence officer to the Canadian Corps of the Second Army who were to cross the valley of the Stroombeek and attack Passchendaele on the 26th. Near the end of October he was given notice to go forward.

Dear Maggie,

I am writing to you with some rather strange news, which you may or may not welcome. I believe that I have evidence that your younger brother Alex is somewhere in the area. In Poperinge there is a type of Christian soldiers' club called Talbot House, which is used by all ranks for recreation. It is quite large, with gardens and a chapel, a tiny library and canteen facilities. Hundreds of men use it each day, sitting about writing letters or playing billiards. Part of the wall on the ground floor is known as Friendship Corner where you can leave your name on a card and say who you wish to contact. I did not tell you this earlier in order not to raise your hopes, but a few weeks ago before being posted to Brigade H2, I put my own name there, asking Alex to make contact if he saw it. I now enclose the card which was left beside mine during the time when I was away. I will make enquiries as best I can but don't expect news soon. Thousands of troops pass through this town so it may prove impossible to trace one soldier. Also, I am going back up the line.

Maggie took the small card which was folded inside Francis's letter and recognized her young brother's handwriting.

I AM FINE. TELL MUM AND DAD AND MAGGIE NOT TO WORRY. ALEX.

Maggie put the card in her apron pocket. This news would have a mixed reception at home. Her mother and father would welcome the news that Alex was still alive, but it also told them that he was in the direct line of fire. She would try to find out which regiments had been in Poperinge recently and see if any of them matched up with the towns where the London train stopped on its journey from Edinburgh. Given time she *would* trace her brother's movements, although her enquiries would now have to wait until the winter campaign ended. At the moment Maggie was concerned for Francis. She reread his letter with that ominous last sentence:

. . . Also, I am going back up the line.

Carrying his maps and latest intelligence reports, Francis made his way forward to join the Canadian Division. His waking nightmares made it hard for him to distinguish between the real and the unreal, and at times on his passage to the front line he was unsure whether he was dreaming or actually seeing the raw horror that the land beyond Ypres had become. The front line was merely joined-up shell-holes which the Canadians fought for one by one as they crawled up to the place known as Crest Farm.

On 10 November the Army finally gained their last objective. Beyond two German pillboxes at the top of a gentle slope Francis unpacked his equipment to plot the co-ordinates which would confirm that they had arrived at the village of Passchendaele. Except that no ruined steeple, flattened house or derelict hut remained to define its presence. The place as such was now merely a map reference. Francis stood with his cartographer's stylus and began to mark down the degrees of latitude and longitude when he was suddenly aware that the lives of thousands of men had been sacrificed in order to bring him to a location which did not exist. Francis looked around him and began to laugh.

And found that he could not stop.

Dear Miss Dundas,

I am writing to you as I know that you have maintained a correspondence with my son Francis, and may be concerned as to his whereabouts and as to why you have not heard from him. At present he is on extended sick leave in England. At the moment he is not well enough to receive letters, but will be in touch with you when he has recovered himself.

Yours sincerely,

Regina Armstrong-Barnes

1918

SPECIAL ORDER OF THE DAY

By Field-Marshal Sir Douglas Haig, K.T., G.C.B., G.C.V.O., K.C.I.E., Commander-In-Chief, British Armies in France.

To ALL RANKS OF THE BRITISH ARMY IN FRANCE AND FLANDERS

Three weeks ago today the enemy began his terrific attacks against us on a fifty-mile front. His objects are to separate us from the French, to take the Channel Ports and destroy the British Army.

In spite of throwing already 106 Divisions into the battle and enduring the most reckless sacrifice of human life, he has as yet made little progress towards his goals.

We owe this to the determined fighting and self-sacrifice of our troops. Words fail me to express the admiration which I feel for the splendid resistance offered by all ranks of our Army under the most trying circumstances.

Many amongst us now are tired. To those I would say that victory will belong to the side which holds out the longest. The French Army is moving rapidly and in great force to our support.

There is no other course open to us but to fight it out! Every position must be held to the last man: there must be no retirement. With our backs to the wall, and believing in the justice of our cause, each one of us must fight on to the end. The safety of our homes and the Freedom of mankind alike depend upon the conduct of each one of us at this critical moment.

D. HAIG,
F.M.,
Commander-in-Chief,
British Armies in France.

General Headquarters,
Thursday, April 11th, 1918.

Chapter 37

ALEX PULLED OFF his gas mask and stopped walking. Eric Kidd's hand was on his arm. 'C'mon, laddie,' he said. 'Remember what I told you. Keep moving.'

'Where are we going?' said Alex.

Eric laughed out loud. 'Dunno. But if we stay here we'll get killed.'

Shells were bursting near to them and the air was filled with smoke and gas.

'Put your mask on,' Eric told Alex gently. 'They're using mustard and that's filthy stuff.'

Beside an abandoned piece of artillery they came across a captain of the Royal Engineers.

'Go back!' he shouted at them. 'Go back! We are overrun.'

Although seriously wounded, he was trying to organize the retreat and direct the men towards Brigade Headquarters. But the gun position was attracting enemy fire and he urged them to leave him. Eric stuffed wadding into the officer's wound and left him, moving back the way they had come.

Among all the other noise Alex did not hear the bullet that killed his friend. He only saw Eric Kidd's head snap forward and his body fall like a puppet with its strings cut. Alex ran to help, but there was nothing he could do. The bullet had gone through the back of Eric's neck. His eyes were closed and there was blood around his mouth. Alex moaned and fell to his knees. He knelt there for a while, rocking backwards and forwards, talking to himself. Through the smoke and fog he could still hear noises; machine-gun fire, and men shouting. He would have to move on, but he did not want to leave Eric lying there, alone and cold. Alex took off his tunic and wrapped it around the head of his friend and then he stumbled away, tears coursing down his face. There was a thunderous roar in his ears and a shell exploded in front of him, throwing up a great fountain of mud. Alex got up, walked a few paces, staggering as he went, fell over, managed to get to his knees, then collapsed into the mud.

When he came to it was almost daylight, a clean bright dawn forcing its way through his slitted eyes. His eyelids seemed glued together and when he raised his hands to his face he realized it was because there was mud caked and congealed across it. He had to spit from his dry throat onto his hands to try to loosen the pale clay and ease his eyelids open with his fingers. He sat up.

In a shell-hole directly in front of him were two German soldiers, and they had seen him. The nearest to him raised his arm and picked up an object which lay beside him. A stick grenade! Alex grabbed the Mills bomb at his belt and pulled the pin off. He stood up and threw it. With a great roar of earth and metal the two men were blasted into the air. The force of the explosion also caught Alex and he stumbled, painfully drawing breath into his raw lungs. When the dirt settled he saw that one of the men was still alive. He had his back to Alex and, although hit in the leg, he was slowly getting to his knees. The man facing him was dead. Alex crawled forward. The dead German in the shell-hole was a man much older than Alex's own father. His helmet had come off and his hair was as white as any grandfather's. Alex had been told that the enemy was so desperately short of manpower that they were drafting old men and children. He was obviously one of their home guard militia, with the black and gold button of the *Landsturm* on his cap. A great surge of elation went through Alex. At last! He had done it, he had killed a Hun! And he was going to kill another. And this time he would see his enemy, face to face, as he did it. He looked for his rifle as the other German rolled round towards him. Now he would be able to say that he had killed one of them with his own hands. He thought of John Malcolm. One Dundas dead, one Dundas to avenge him. His brother's blood was on this soldier's hands, and Alex would make him pay its cost.

The German soldier half turned, and then, crippled by the wound in his leg, he slumped against the side of the shell-hole. Alex could see his face clearly. He was a boy of no more than sixteen years.

Alex grabbed his Lee Enfield rifle, but it was useless, clogged with mud. He would have to stick this soldier with his bayonet. He held his rifle out, the bayonet rigid, as they had been taught in training.

The boy gave a terrible groan and opened his eyes.

Alex thrust his bayonet under the German's throat. The eyes of the two boy soldiers met.

Alex tightened his grip on his rifle. He knew what would happen now. He had heard stories from his fellow soldiers who had captured enemy trenches. The enemy would recognize his uniform and try to beg for mercy. '*Kamerad*,' he would plead, '*Kamerad*.'

Alex braced himself. As soon as the German spoke he would jab him in the throat. Like sticking a turnip, the training officer had said: 'A turnip, remember. Not a tomato, or an orange. The Hun has a lot of bone and gristle. Put your shoulder behind it, hard as you can. Straight in and straight out again.'

But the boy said nothing. He looked at Alex, turned his head to the side and closed his eyes.

His neck was exposed. Alex swallowed the bile from the back of his own throat. He stared at the boy awaiting death by his hand. Then with a quick movement Alex flung his rifle from him, crouched down onto the earth and put his head in his hands.

After a time, Alex pushed the German with his foot. The boy opened his eyelids slowly. His eyes swivelled round to look at Alex, but still he did not speak. Alex took his water bottle and held it out. The boy looked at it without interest.

'Water,' said Alex. 'Are you thirsty?'

The boy didn't reply. Alex took a drink himself and offered his water bottle again. The boy's eyes were dulled. Alex knew that look; he recognized the blanked-out expression of a soldier who had given up. Eventually Alex shuffled across the space between them. He put his arm around the boy's shoulder to support him, cupped the water bottle to the boy's lips and helped him drink. Then he lay back down on the earth and fell asleep.

Chapter 38

HUGH KANE'S MOTHER turned the small package over and over in her hands before eventually opening it. She looked at the contents in complete bewilderment. Then she went to the kitchen cupboard and took down the box of African ebony wood. She placed the regimental badge – a horn surmounted by a crown – and the scraps of torn and bloodstained letters inside, closed the lid, and returned the box to its place on the shelf. It was still in her thoughts later as she prepared to go out. The pram, which she used to collect her daily washing, stood ready in the hall and she had to squeeze past it to gather her outdoor clothes from the peg behind the door. Hat and coat in hand, she stared at the empty pram. Then she went back through to the kitchen, took the ebony box from the cupboard, and sat down heavily in her chair. Minutes passed. The fire burned and she watched the coals shift and settle. Then she lifted the lid of the box and began to look for the birth certificate of her child, Kenneth, who had died before he was two. The birth certificate which she knew would not be there.

'*Soldaten*.' Alex heard an urgent whisper in his ear. The German boy had shaken him awake. Alex started up and the boy put his finger to his lips and pointed. Beyond the edge of the shell-hole was a road, and the road was busy with German troops and armoury streaming westwards. The German boy pointed again, this time to a deep ditch a few yards away. Alex started to crawl towards it. To his surprise the boy followed him.

From his hiding place Alex watched the road. The Allies must have fallen right back, as nothing seemed to be hindering this rapid German advance. Alex decided it would be safer to move away from here, and as it got dark he began to crawl along the ditch. Again, the German boy followed. Eventually they reached the outskirts of a tiny ruined village away from any main road. Alex had no idea where he was, or in which direction he should go. He knew that he was somewhere near the river Somme. This was the same area where John Malcolm had been killed, and when he'd first heard that he was coming here he had been glad, thinking at one time that he might even kill the German who had killed his brother. Weeks ago they had passed through the British base in a French town which had a cathedral with a broken statue of the Virgin Mary. He remembered vaguely that it was a man's name, and by the movement of the sun in the sky he thought that it lay west of here. But if the German Army had moved forward so quickly then that town was probably taken by now. It would be better, Alex decided, to remain where he was.

In the remains of the little village he found a ransacked army billet. Most of the stock had been plundered but there was clothing and enough stores for both him and the boy to live on. Alex thought that the village itself might be unsafe and decided to make a base in the ditch. All his play-acting in the woods around Stratharden proved useful as he constructed his den. The German boy's name was Kurt and despite his injured leg he tried to help as much as he could. Alex went foraging, dragging materials from the fields, some corkscrew barbed-wire supports, a rubberized gas curtain, and any wood that he could find. He had to concede that, despite not being able to move about much, Kurt was better at making the actual shelter than he was. When it was finished they piled earth on top. Spotter planes came over at regular intervals and although the ditch was fairly deep Alex wanted to make sure that their hide would attract no attention. He took everything he could carry from the abandoned billet, including a bottle of whisky and some cigarettes which he found under a pile of rubble. They opened army rations tins and ate the food cold.

Summer began to creep across the devastated land. The weather became less cold, but at night the boys still huddled together for warmth. Alex found English magazines and books in the village and he read these in the evenings, often out loud to Kurt. He didn't think the German boy understood much but he seemed to like the sound of Alex's voice, and it helped him fall asleep. As the weeks went by Alex began to think that he could stay here for ever; he might learn to trap rabbits, even find a river and fish. The rest of the world had lost its reason and this place was pleasant, the sun was now hot during the day and they spent a great part of it sitting outside. Alex felt his mind begin a slow release from agitation. He slept a great deal, and as he slept, his dreams became less troubled by images of death and killing. The sound of guns and gunfire was ever present, but Alex shut off any thoughts of reality beyond his immediate survival. Perhaps he could just wait until the War ended and go back home?

And then Kurt became ill. Alex had known for some time that there was something wrong with the German boy's leg. He had tried to dress it as best he could, but the one thing that he had not found anywhere in the village was medical supplies. The bleeding had stopped, but the wound had never healed, and as time went on a trickly red rust discharge leaked from under the bandage. Kurt was also becoming slightly delirious. Alex didn't leave his side, forcing him to eat and drink, washing his face, and changing his soiled clothes. One day Alex woke to find the boy pallid, his breathing faint, his eyes rolling back in his head.

'I am going to find medicine,' he said loudly in Kurt's ear, and he ran off to the village.

There was nothing there of any use to him. Alex searched through each ruined building looking more thoroughly than he had done previously. No first-aid pack, no disinfectant, nothing. Alex became desperate, scrabbling about among the rubble. He had seen the effects of gangrene on wounded soldiers. Without antiseptic Kurt would die. Finally, in the billet Alex lifted another bottle of whisky. It would be useful to help clean out the wound, or Kurt could drink it and it might ease the pain. He was just about to step back into the street when there was a clatter of an engine and a lorry with troops came lurching towards him. The soldiers were in a uniform which he didn't recognize, although he knew it was neither British nor French. One wore a hat which fluted to a point at the top. Alex's stomach flipped over. It must be the famous and terrible Prussian Guards! He crept into the shadow of a wall and watched them. They were too far away for him to hear what they were saying, but by the drift of the voices he knew they were not English. Alex's throat tightened with fear. Another van arrived and he could see clearly what they were doing. This vehicle had a red cross on the side. They were setting up a medical aid station.

Alex padded silently backwards and crouched low. In a moment he would slip away and get safely back to his den in the ditch. He thought about the German boy lying there. He, Alex, could live for another month or so, or even longer, out of doors, but Kurt would not survive. Kurt's best hope was with the German doctors whom Alex could see unloading their supplies. But Alex knew that if he gave himself up he might be shot. At the very least he could be taken prisoner. He might become one of those soldiers who disappeared and were never found. His parents would read his name in the casualty lists . . . *Missing, believed killed.*

Alex thought again about Kurt. Without medical help Kurt would surely die. Should he let this happen? It would be revenge for John Malcolm's death. Once it had been his sworn vow to kill a German and avenge his brother. But he had already killed a German, the older man who had been with Kurt in the shell-hole, and it had only made him feel scared and unhappy. Eric Kidd had been right when he'd said that revenge wasn't an answer. It prevented him from remembering his big brother in the way that he should. And now he had seen the effects of war; on soldiers, on civilians, on animals, and on the land, and he was sick of it. And Kurt wasn't just a German, he was a German with a name, a person.

Alex carefully placed the stolen bottle of whisky down onto the ground and stood up. Then he walked out from his hiding place with his hands above his head.

Chapter 39

IN AUGUST 1918 Maggie received a letter from her father.

My dearest daughter,

It is with a heart full of sorrow that I write you. We believe that your brother Alex is now lost to us. Some time ago, Mrs Kane, Edward's mother, had received word from the War Office that a soldier named Kenneth Kane was missing, believed killed, in the action that took place around the French town of Albert in the Spring of this year. She assumed that they'd made a mistake with the address and thought no more of it. Recently they returned to her a regimental badge and letters, saying that these had been in a bloodstained tunic found with a group of dead soldiers when the final push forward was being made over the ground lost earlier this year. They were the only personal items recovered from the belongings of the soldier known as Kenneth Kane. When she read the letters she realized they were from John Malcolm to Alex, and discovered that the birth certificate of her middle son Kenneth who had died in infancy was missing. We think Alex must have taken it and used it to show himself to be of age to join up. We now know why we could not trace him before. He used Kenneth Kane's birth certificate and covered himself being below height for his age by joining a Bantam Battalion. He must have left the train at Durham, for the badge is of the Durham Light Infantry. Enquiries we have made place his battalion in the section that was overrun at the time of the German breakthrough in April. We know of course that mix-ups can happen. His body has not been found and there is a chance that he may be a prisoner, but during the years of this War little joy has come to those who cling to that hope. The officer I spoke to at the Military Barracks told me all was confusion at that time. Those wounded or killed lay where they fell and many of the dead have never been recovered. Alex was last seen among a small group who were trapped in a shell-hole under heavy fire. It would seen therefore that Alex has had his wish. He has gone to be with his brother.

Maggie had to go to her room and lie down. Alex, the baby of the family, was almost certainly dead. Everyone in the hospital knew what had happened in the months of the German breakthrough. The Front around the Somme had almost broken and only by swift retreat had the Allies managed to recover and regroup. Thousands of soldiers had been caught behind the enemy lines. She stared at the ceiling above her bed and raged against the War and those who had caused it. This collective madness had destroyed her two brothers.

With the letter still in her hand Maggie went to see the Matron. She knew that now she must go home. She said a tearful goodbye to Charlotte, wrote quickly to Francis care of his mother, and set off for England.

At the ports on both sides of the Channel the sight of so many soldiers in different uniforms, and the tons of supplies waiting to be sent to the Front, should have cheered her, but it didn't. She now only thought of the thousands of American young men who would die before the War was over. It was clear that it was to be fought to the finish. Both sides seemed determined to wear each other down until there was no-one left. It would be complete attrition, as Francis had predicted in 1916. On her long journey home everyone had a story about the War. They said that in Germany the people were dying of starvation and strikes and riots were commonplace, that their navy would soon mutiny and their army rebel against the Kaiser. It would only be a few weeks and then it would be over and the Allies would win.

If it could be called winning, Maggie thought sadly.

In Stratharden everything was strange, and yet she had been away for little more than a year. Life in France had the harsh reality of groaning wounded men and the constant smell of blood and death. But Maggie now felt as though she had been protected from the reality of another life. Here there was the day-by-day coping with restrictions and rations, the ever-present sense of controlled grief and the anxiety of grief to come. Neither of her parents spoke openly of the loss of their two sons, but Maggie's own mind echoed with thoughts of her brothers. Alex's boots still stood by the back door, John Malcolm's letters were a crumpled package on the sideboard. Their bodies now lay in the soil of a foreign country and she had no-one to speak to, nowhere to go to grieve for them. Her lack of communication with Francis had created a cavity within her. She felt incomplete. Without the hospital routine she was unsettled, and unable to relax. She better understood Francis's reluctance to take leave and, when he did, his impatience to be back with his unit.

Within her own home there had been a subtle shift in the balance of the household. Had her father changed so much, or did she now view him differently? Her recollection of him was of an opinionated, almost pompous, dapper man. He seemed nearly completely broken down and worked mainly in the back of the shop away from any contact with his customers. He was less voluble, less assured in his observations on the state of the world. Her mother, although still physically frail, still self-effacing, seemed more quietly in control. She spoke to Maggie's father firmly, encouraging him to dress and shave every day. In the morning her mother did up his collar studs for him, her father standing passively while this was done. And once, Maggie saw her mother use the flat of her hand to brush down the front of his suit, as she had done to John Malcolm before he set out for school each morning – her twin as a little boy usually having bits of his breakfast scattered on his pullover. Maggie turned away quickly before the ache in her heart began to swell again.

Maggie knew that she must make some purpose of her future. The shop was being more than adequately run by Willie, with some part-time help. The barefoot boy from the poorer end of the village was now a young lad who could manage the daily sales. He was obviously relieved when Maggie told him she had no intention of returning to work there full time, that she would help with the book-keeping, but intended to do volunteer work at Stratharden House until all the patients were ready to go home. Later she went into Edinburgh and made enquiries about courses in further education. The War did indeed seem to be drawing to a close, and she had no intention of returning to the life she had lived before it began.

In late October, as Germany's Allies collapsed and Britain prepared for victory, a letter came from Francis's mother in London.

My son's health continues to be poor and he has been invalided out of the Army. He will convalesce in Bournemouth as he needs to spend some time recuperating before returning to Stratharden. He asks me to let you know that he is in an unfit state to impose his company on anyone at the moment.

Maggie curbed her instinct to reply that she would see Francis in any state he saw fit to present himself. Instead, she wrote to say that the sea air would do him good and she looked forward to seeing him.

On the morning of Monday 11 November she was going over accounts in the shop when the letterbox rattled on the shuttered door. It was Eddie Kane's mother.

'It's nearly eleven o'clock,' she told Maggie. 'Come and listen for the Armistice bells.' And as Maggie hesitated, the older woman put her arm around the girl's shoulders and led her outside.

Some villagers were travelling to Edinburgh to join in the Armistice celebrations but Maggie had turned down an invitation to go with them. There would be fireworks and speeches and bands and cheering crowds, but she knew that this would make her sad beyond bearing. Her spirit was with the men and women in Belgium and France. She'd rather take part in the street party which was to be the village's own quieter celebration later. Most of her family's friends and neighbours had stayed at home: Stratharden had lost too many of its sons for there to be any flamboyant noisy celebration today. She stood close to Mrs Kane and saw all down the main road people waiting by their front door or gathering together in little groups. As the church bells began to ring to signal the ceasefire the sense of relief was tangible, people shook hands and hugged each other. Maggie looked up and saw her parents at the upstairs window. They were leaning against each other and both of them were crying. She was glad that they had attained some kind of release. Maggie thought of Francis somewhere in England, and Charlotte in France. She silently prayed for her two brothers reunited in death, then she returned to the shop and went on with her work.

Chapter 40

CHARLOTTE CAME HOME, stopping in London to meet up with her mother and brother, the three of them travelling to Stratharden together. Her friendship with Maggie was unchanged. She came to the shop and often had tea with Maggie's mother. Sometimes she would ask Maggie's father to accompany her part of the way home, and would take his arm quite naturally as they walked together.

Prisoners of war were being released and shipped back to Britain. Although neither Alex's nor Kenneth Kane's name had ever appeared on any list of captives, if a ship was due to land at Leith, Maggie would always make the journey through to Edinburgh to wait by the dockside. She did this more out of a sense of duty than entertaining any real hope that Alex might be there. Sometimes Charlotte would go with her, and it was on one of these journeys together that she told Maggie of her intention to go back to France.

‘The flu epidemic has caused a nursing shortage, and I have need of some occupation.’

Maggie thought of Charlotte’s use of the word ‘occupation’. Scarcely two years ago it would have been an incongruous statement for her to make. If there had been no war then Charlotte’s future would have been constrained by her social circumstances; her achievement would have been to marry into a good family. As for herself, this war had changed her life the way a river might alter course after a landslide. She did not dress, speak, act, or even think as she had done previously. Her reading and consequent self-awareness would make her seek new challenges, her experiences had given her the confidence to face the responsibilities that these might bring.

‘I’d like to find John Malcolm’s burial place,’ Charlotte went on. ‘There are people in France who are trying to take care of the war cemeteries. I know that I will find his grave near where he fell, around Beaumont Hamel where the Twenty-Ninth Division fought. I hope that there are green fields around . . .’ her voice began to break, ‘with a river close by.’

Maggie held Charlotte’s hands. ‘Put flowers there for me,’ she said.

‘You are so like him,’ said Charlotte. ‘That day on the bridge, when you came to tell me of his death, the sun was on your hair. It was the same colour as his the day we said goodbye.' She wiped the tears away. 'Some days I feel good about how he went. He'll never change for me now, always laughing, happy, bright . . . Not crushed by circumstance.' She looked at Maggie. 'My brother carries it all within him.'

Maggie thought of how she had first met Francis on his return. A little group of villagers had gathered as he and his mother and sister had descended from the bus. She saw him to be frighteningly thin, his face around his eyes crosshatched with tight lines. He had stood awkwardly in the street as people came and shook his hand. Embarrassed, Maggie had hugged him briefly, and he, under the eye of the village and cautious of her reaction, had been reserved, formally polite. How strange and distant they were with each other after the night in the supply hut of the hospital at Rienne.

Charlotte had told Maggie that Francis rarely ventured from the house but Maggie had caught sight of him out walking once or twice. This had upset her. He had need of her when the War was being fought. Now that it was over he seemed to need her no more. Finally Maggie decided to send him a letter, and do as she had always done, write her own truth.

Dear Francis,

I hope that you are well. I worry that you are not. Please let me know how you are.

Maggie

Then she added a postscript.

I miss our letters.

The next evening, alone in the shop she was adding up the weekly orders when she heard someone whisper her name.

'*Maggie.*'

She looked up from the account book. Francis was standing in front of her.

Maggie undid the strings on her apron and took it off slowly. She folded it carefully and laid it on the counter between them.

'I have lost my judgement of what is, and what is not.' He spoke with difficulty. 'I am unsure of almost everything.'

'I am constant,' she replied.

'I could never say anything before, never declare myself. It would have been too cruel, to create a bond that might have been destroyed.'

Maggie nodded. Like a spring uncoiling with relief, she breathed out, as if she had been holding her breath for a long time and could only now let it go.

Francis leaned across the counter, and with both hands outstretched he gripped her shoulders. He kissed her, and she took his mouth onto hers and held him there, body and soul, existing only in that moment of time.

He stepped backwards and looked keenly into her face. 'You do love me, then?'

'Yes,' she said, as though she'd known it all of her life.

Chapter 41

TOWARDS THE END of November, Charlotte, who walked to the bridge nearly every morning before breakfast, met the post boy on his way up the drive. He handed her a letter, touched his cap, and cycled away without a word. Charlotte turned the black-edged envelope over in her hand. It was addressed to Annie, the housekeeper. When Charlotte returned to the house Annie was serving her mother breakfast in the morning room.

'Annie,' Charlotte said gently. 'I met the post boy when I was out. There is a letter for you.'

Charlotte's mother put her knife down. She looked quickly at Charlotte. 'Annie,' she said. 'Perhaps you would like some privacy to read this alone.'

Annie shook her head and took a step backwards. 'No.' She spoke to Charlotte. 'Give it to your mother. She will read it for me.'

Charlotte saw her mother's face turn pale. Mrs Armstrong-Barnes took the envelope, opened it, and spread out the folded piece of paper flat on the table in front of her. She began to read the words very slowly. 'I am commanded by . . .' Charlotte's mother stopped reading. She raised her head and looked directly at her housekeeper. 'Annie,' she said, 'your boys are dead. Rory and Ewan's bodies have now been found. It is believed that they were killed on the day they went missing in 1915.'

'Oh, Annie,' Charlotte whispered. 'I am so sorry.'

'As am I,' said Charlotte's mother, in a strange, strangled voice.

Annie looked at her. 'They are definitely gone?'

Charlotte's mother recovered herself. 'Yes.' She said the words purposively, so that there could be no mistake. 'Their bodies have now been positively identified. Both of them are now officially designated as killed in action.'

'I'd always hoped . . .' Annie couldn't finish the sentence. She took the edge of her apron to wipe her eyes, which were curiously dry.

And Charlotte suddenly had a clear memory of the old couple who had arrived at the hospital in France to visit their son who had died the day before their arrival. They had the same stunned look as Annie had now. The boy's mother, dry-eyed, bewildered, reaching for her handkerchief in her small purse of soft lilac lace, saying to the Matron, 'Lady, I knew that he was grievously wounded, but I had hoped . . .'

'I had hoped . . .' The same words Annie had just spoken.

But now there was no hope. No hope for them, no hope for Annie, no hope for her, Charlotte. And as her mind tried to encompass the concept, Charlotte knew that in times like this there was no difference in class or wealth or religion or race; that people cried, and wept, and broke with sorrow – in Britain and in France, in Belgium and Russia, and in Germany too.

Charlotte pressed her hands to her head. It was too much. This great collective grief was swamping the whole world she knew. Every home was flooding with inconsolable lamentations. On the street, in villages and towns, people met and passed each other and barely nodded their heads. There was nothing they could say to each other, there was nothing to say. In the shop, John Malcolm's mother smiled a welcome with eyes that were elsewhere. Her face composed, her hands restless, plucking at her clothes. Charlotte shook her head as if trying to rid herself of these images. She needed to talk to Francis. Francis, who had understood this from the beginning. Those angry outbursts when reading the newspapers; he had seen it all to come, had known what would happen.

And, as if he had heard her thoughts, the door opened and Francis entered. Annie gathered herself and moved quickly past him.

'What's amiss?' said Francis. He looked after Annie as she left the room, and then back to Charlotte in alarm. He hurried across to his sister and led her to a chair, where he sat her down and began to stroke her hair, and soothe her with baby talk. 'There, there,' he said. 'I'm here. It's all right. Your big brother is here.'

'But it isn't all right, Francis!' Charlotte cried. 'And it never will be now!' And she began to cry great gulping sobs, all her unspent mourning for John Malcolm pouring out. The sadness of the joy of all the times they'd had and that were gone for ever, the despair of everything now denied to them, the things that would never be.

Francis signalled his mother to bring some brandy and between them they managed to calm Charlotte. His mother told him of Annie's telegram. Francis said nothing, only bowed his head and put his face in his hands.

It was left to Charlotte's mother to see to the running of the house for the rest of the morning and it was she who prepared lunch, took some to Annie, and insisted that Francis and Charlotte eat something with her.

'Francis,' she said when they were almost finished. 'There is something I want you to do this afternoon. There is to be a party in the village hall to celebrate the end of the War, and I think it is your place to represent this house.'

'A party?' said Francis in disbelief. 'You want *me* to attend a party today to celebrate our victory?'

'I see no reason why you should not,' said his mother severely.

'I could give you very many reasons why not.'

'This is not the time nor the place, Francis,' his mother said in a warning voice.

Francis felt his hands begin to tremble and he pressed them together. 'Tell me why I should then,' he demanded.

'Leadership, Francis,' said his mother. 'Leadership.'

Francis threw back his head and laughed. It was a hard, humourless sound. 'Please do not talk to me about leadership, Mother. I became a leader. I led men to their death, day after day.'

His mother was unflinching. 'I am talking about our place in this community. I would like you to represent me at the village celebrations.'

'Why don't you go?'

His mother screwed up her napkin. 'I am uneasy about going myself. I suppose I feel guilty that you both returned safe and . . .' there was the slightest pause, '. . . well.'

Francis smiled, but his voice shook. 'Mother, I am as well as any decent human being might be after taking part in such a war. Personally I think that it is those who try to justify this war who should be locked up in an insane asylum. Do remember that I had these strange ideas before I went out to France. Being at the Front only confirmed what I already believed.'

'You could at least allow yourself to rejoice in the fact that it's over,' his mother said sharply.

'Mother has a point,' said Charlotte quietly.

Francis raised his eyebrows. He opened his mouth to reply but at that moment there was a quick knock and Annie entered. She was dressed for going out.

She spoke to Charlotte's mother. 'I'd like the rest of the day off, ma'am.'

Charlotte's mother half rose from her chair. 'Of course you may,' she said. 'Take whatever time you need.' She looked to Francis. 'You will drive Annie in the car if there are relatives she has to visit.'

'That won't be necessary, I can walk to where I'm going,' said Annie. She adjusted her hatpin and secured her hat more firmly on her head. 'The village party is today, and I intend to be there.'

There was a silence, from which Charlotte was the first to recover.

'How very brave of you, Annie,' she said quietly.

'The way I look at it is,' said Annie, 'my boys would have wanted to celebrate the Peace. They can't be there, so I'm going for them.'

Francis got up and crossed the room. He offered his arm to Annie. 'Would you allow an ex-soldier to escort you there?'

Charlotte looked at her mother. 'Perhaps we should all walk down?' she suggested.

Charlotte thought later that it was the children who had really made it worthwhile, as they charged about amongst the chairs and around the long tables with the adults prepared to allow them their freedom. They gave meaning to the bunting and the flags. But afterwards she was tired and needed some solitude, so that when Francis asked if he might walk her home she declined.

'I would prefer my own company,' she told him. 'When I take that walk I remember John Malcolm. I will sit on the bridge for a little while.' She sighed. 'It seems so long ago now. I was such a child then.'

'And of course now you are a mature woman,' Francis teased her.

'We certainly grew up very quickly,' said Maggie, siding with Charlotte.

'There is something quite terrible about the death of so many young people,' said Francis, after Charlotte had left. 'By the end of the War, more than half the Army was under nineteen years old. The old die, and we are accustomed to that. It is almost a proper thing. They signify the past which slips away, as it should. But the death of youth denies us what might have come. Our present is obliterated and our future altered irrevocably.'

'I was thinking that if I have children,' said Maggie, 'they will never know John Malcolm as their uncle. My twin brother will become the one who died in the Great War. His personal identity has been taken from him. He will be their mother's brother, the one who was killed at the Somme.'

Francis slipped his arm through Maggie's own. 'Your brother went to his death believing he fought for his country. Charlotte told me of John Malcolm's letters. They are full of enthusiasm.'

'Wasn't there any glory in it at all for you?' Maggie asked him.

Francis looked Maggie full in the face. 'Yes, and that is the most awful part of it all for me. Seduced by tales of derring-do, I ran across the benighted piece of land that separated us from them, hoping to kill or be killed. I went with all the others, shell-fire roaring in our ears, exhilarated when we reached the other side.'

'But there *were* many acts of bravery.'

'Do deeds of heroism justify the cause?' said Francis.

Maggie wondered if she would ever completely understand this complex man.

'Would you return to nursing?' he asked her, as they walked together towards the shop.

'Not nursing, no,' said Maggie. 'Charlotte is more of a nurse than I. She is calm and kind, and yet there is fine mettle beneath that.'

'Are you thinking of going back to help your father in the shop?' Francis persisted gently.

'Not the shop. No. Willie has all the makings of a general manager. If you listened to him he would extend it halfway down the street. He'll have it expanded into a three-floor emporium in a few years,' said Maggie. She thought for a moment and then said, 'I would like to study. I've applied to work in one of the city libraries, and I plan to attend a night school of some kind in order to obtain higher certificates.

University College in London is offering a new course leading to a Diploma in Librarianship. I would like to do some work which helps spread the use of books. It appeals to both my organizing skills and my belief that Knowledge, more than anything else, can overcome oppression.'

'Would you have time to write to me?' Francis asked carefully.

'Francis, I would be bereft if we did not sustain our relationship.'

He took her hand. 'I would like us to have an understanding, so that in time I might speak to your father.'

Maggie smiled. 'On the understanding,' she said, 'that first you speak to me.'

Francis drew her closer to him. 'It has taken me time to appreciate that we were linked by more than my piteous need and your charity. To find both solace and stimulation within such beauty seemed to me a miracle that I could scarcely lay claim to.'

They had reached the entrance of the shop and Maggie stopped at the doorway. Francis leaned across and blocked her way inside. 'I cannot imagine a life without you.' His voice was thick in his throat and his eyes met hers. He put one hand on each side of her face. 'That which I hold, I adore,' he whispered, and he bent his head and kissed her.

After a moment they drew apart. The sky had darkened towards evening. Maggie looked up at the bright points of starlight which were appearing. 'And that is by way of being a small miracle also,' she said.

Francis kissed the top of her head and stepped into the roadway.

A young man in a private's uniform was walking slowly down the street towards the shop. 'He's rather late for the celebrations,' said Maggie.

On seeing her the boy's step quickened, and she screwed up her eyes to watch him approach. 'I suppose we could find a bit of cake for him.'

'He looks very weary, as if he's walked all the way from Edinburgh,' said Francis.

Maggie took a step forward and her hand clutched at her throat. 'Oh my God,' she said softly.

Francis turned to look at her stricken face. 'What is it?' he asked.

'It's my brother,' Maggie gasped. 'It's my brother Alex.'

Chapter 42

MAGGIE'S CRIES COULD be heard several streets away, and her family and neighbours came running at once. The boy Willie, thinking Maggie was being attacked, appeared brandishing a broom bigger than himself.

Maggie ran to Alex and they hugged each other, she weeping, and he, almost breaking down, caught between laughter and crying. Then he set her aside gently, and pushed his way through the crowd until he found his mother. She clasped her arms around his neck. 'My son,' she sobbed, 'my baby. My son, Alex, my son, my son . . .'

Someone ran and fetched a chair so that she could sit down, and then all the neighbours had to shake Alex by the hand. Many were in tears. It took an age before they managed to usher Alex inside.

Francis quietly took his leave of Maggie and slipped away.

Eventually Alex was upstairs and seated in his father's chair by the fireside. Maggie's father stood with his back to the fire, but every few minutes he walked around the room so that he could ruffle his son's hair or pat his shoulder.

Maggie was perched on the arm of the chair, and her mother sat at her son's feet on a low stool holding his plate with a piece of cake on it. Alex was clumsily trying to manage a cup of tea with a saucer. At intervals his mother took her son's free hand in her own and stroked it, or lifted it to her lips and pressed it against her cheek.

'I must go and see Mrs Kane and ask her to forgive me for taking Kenneth's birth certificate,' Alex said, after a while.

'She was in the street,' said Maggie. 'I spoke to her. She is happy to see you home.'

Alex looked at his parents and at Maggie. 'I am sorry for the worry I must have caused you all. I can only say that at the time it seemed to me to be the right thing to do, to go and take revenge for my brother.'

'John Malcolm had a peaceful death, son,' said Maggie's father. 'We had word from a soldier who was there when he died.'

There was a silence, and then Alex said, 'I saw him, you know. I never told anyone about it, but on the day the War Office telegram arrived here, I saw him out in the back lane. He was smiling at me.'

A sob came from his mother's throat, and Alex stretched out and laid his hand on the top of her head.

'I held this idea of vengeance in my heart. And at the beginning that was enough to keep me going, but . . .' Alex's voice slowed. 'I came to realize that killing can sicken the soul.'

Maggie nodded. Soldiers she had nursed in France shared this sentiment.

Alex continued with his story. 'Then my unit was caught in the German spring breakthrough. I was cut off with another lad . . .' Alex hesitated. His last news of Kurt was that he was recovering after having his leg amputated. Alex looked around at the faces of his family. He would wait until their wounds of grief had healed some before telling them the full story of his last days of the War. 'Eventually I was found by some ANZAC troops,' he went on, 'the Australians and New Zealanders. I didn't recognize their accent and when I saw the New Zealand army hat at first I thought they were Germans. They took me with them, and it was months before I got back down the line.'

'Why didn't you telegraph when you got back to Britain?' asked his father.

'I only got back to my base in England yesterday and there they told me that you had been sent word that I was probably dead. The Sergeant reckoned I'd get here as soon as any telegram and gave me leave to go home.' Alex leaned forward and there were tears in his eyes as he spoke to his mother. 'I dreamed of it every night, Ma. Every single night I imagined how it would be when I came home.' He looked around the room. 'The fire burning in the chimney, you in your chair, Dad standing as he is now in front of the mantelpiece. The table set for tea. I would make up conversations in my head. What you would say, how I would reply. Night after night I did it. It helped to keep me going.'

Then there were tears, and tears, and more tears, and after a while Alex stretched his legs, winked at Maggie, and said jokingly, 'If I'd known I was coming home to all this crying, I'd have stayed where I was. I thought there'd be some laughter here. I got plenty of sadness in France.'

There was a sudden silence and Maggie's mother turned terrible eyes to Alex, searching her son's face. 'Was it the hell that some people say it was?'

Maggie noticed that her father, standing in front of the fire, had become quite still. And it struck Maggie suddenly what she had been turning over and over in her mind in the last hour. In that it *was* Alex sitting in front of her, returned from the Great War, assuredly it was . . . and yet it wasn't. Her brother had changed in some irrevocable way, although she couldn't place what was different, his eyes, the lines about his mouth? His way of holding himself had altered; the act of placing his hand on his mother's head, he comforting her, made Maggie realize that her younger brother was a boy no more.

'Was it very bad, son?' her father asked gravely.

Alex hesitated; he caught Maggie's eye. 'Not so bad . . .' he said lightly, '. . . you know . . .'

And between their parents, brother and sister looked at each other, and then looked away.

'It would have been cruel to tell them the full truth. Was it such a terrible lie?' Maggie asked Francis.

It was a few weeks later and they were making their way to the official dedication of the village's War Memorial. Mrs Armstrong-Barnes had donated a piece of land which had been planted with wild flowers and herbs, primroses, violets, and rosemary for remembrance. Even Francis had to agree that this seemed appropriate. The little park would be a place for relatives and friends to come and visit; a focus for remembering the fallen, lying far from home in marked and unmarked graves.

'What *is* the full truth?' asked Francis. 'Inhuman conditions and appalling waste of life? That was certainly the case. But for many it was a glorious death. A noble calling, a man marching away to do his duty to protect his mother, wife, children. That's what we are bred to do – that *is* our duty. And there is glamour there too, the allure of the uniform, the camaraderie of men together, and the great good *fun* it could be in the village billets behind the lines.'

Maggie caught a glimmer of the torment of this man's soul, for whom nothing was black and white, only infinite shades of grey. 'You sound almost as though you enjoyed parts of it.'

'Everyone experienced that at certain times,' said Francis. 'The sense of relief when you saw the next set of men coming to take over from you, the great joy of knowing that you had come safely through another tour of duty at the Front. The swelling, overwhelming pride of handing over your position intact, of being able to say that you had held the line in your sector. The latter gave a feeling almost of victory. That is why the French Army was bled white at Verdun. Their honour, and the honour of France rested with them. "*Ils ne passeront pas!*" they cried, day after day . . . and the Germans never did. So now every Frenchman feels that he fought and won with General Petain at Verdun.'

'You think these are not genuine feelings?' said Maggie.

Francis smiled a weary smile. 'My point is that they are. And, God help me, I felt them too. There was tremendous exhilaration, a rush of emotions such as I have never known. This liberating feeling when, exhausted, you captured an objective, and ultimately for me the terrible seduction of successful leadership. I commanded men to follow me – and they did. The awful fact of the matter was that Major Grant was right. Despite withering machine-gun fire and with shells dropping among them, I knew that if I turned my head, the ones left alive would be right alongside me.'

Maggie slipped a hand through his arm. 'You feel corrupted. You who opposed the War do not want to see any glory in it.'

'You are very astute, Maggie,' said Francis. He tucked her arm firmly under his own. 'Do you still have my letters?'

'And all the drawings.'

'If you would lend them back to me I will write an account of what I saw and did. It will serve as some sort of record for the future.'

They went to meet Charlotte who was standing to one side with a bunch of rosemary in her hand. From where she stood Charlotte could see the river and the bridge where she and John Malcolm had said goodbye those years ago. She was glad that her last image of him was his handsome happy face smiling at her. It was something that she could keep inside to help her through the years ahead. She was glad too that John Malcolm's name was carved on the town's War Memorial.

Having his name there meant that there was somewhere to visit and lay flowers, a place to remember . . . to remember every one of them . . . Annie's two boys, Rory and Ewan, Helen's young man, the gardener's lad, the stable boy, the fifteen men and boys from the village who had joined up on the same day and died together, Eddie Kane and all the others.

Charlotte raised her head when the minister began to read out the list of names. As he reached the name of John Malcolm Dundas, without letting go of Francis's arm, Maggie reached out and took Charlotte's hand.

Do you remember the stretcher-cases lurching back
With dying eyes and lolling heads – those ashen-grey
Masks of the lads who once were keen and kind and gay?

Have you forgotten yet? . . .
Look up, and swear by the green of the spring that you'll
never forget.

Siegfried Sassoon,
from 'Aftermath' (March 1919)

About the Author

THERESA BRESLIN is the critically acclaimed, popular author of over fifty books covering every age range and a variety of genres. Her work has been adapted for television, stage and radio, translated worldwide, and won many book prizes – including the prestigious Carnegie Medal for *Whispers in the Graveyard*.

On its first publication *Remembrance* was a bestseller.

She has written eight other historical novels, including *Ghost Soldier* a WWI story for middle school children.

Find out more about Theresa at www.theresabreslin.co.uk or follow her online @TheresaBreslin1

Also available in this series

The day the First World War broke out, Alfie's father promised he wouldn't go away to fight – but he broke that promise, and never came home. Four years later, Alfie is determined to find him . . .

It is tough being the youngest, 'plainest' and naughtiest daughter of a large family – as Victoria Strangeway knows all too well. A fictionalized autobiography of the author's childhood, this is a poignant and vivid picture of life in the build-up to war.